BACKYARD DRAGON

by Betsy and Samuel Sterman

ILLUSTRATIONS BY DAVID WENZEL

SCHOLASTIC INC.
New York Toronto London Auckland Sydney

ISBN 0-590-20834-9

Text copyright © 1993 by Betsy Sterman and Samuel Sterman. Illustrations copyright © 1993 by David Wenzel. All rights reserved. Published by Scholastic Inc., 555 Broadway, New York, NY 10012, by arrangement with HarperCollins Children's Books, a division of HarperCollins Publishers.

12 11 10 9 8 7 6 5 4 3 2 1   4 5 6 7 8 9/9

Printed in the U.S.A.   40

First Scholastic printing, November 1994

For David and Sarah,
with love,
and the hope that
all your dragons will
be small ones.

1

OWEN SQUINTED AGAINST THE thin November sun and watched his huge box kite rise on the wind.

It worked!

The kids in school wouldn't laugh at him now. He'd heard their mocking voices after he had talked about building a kite like this. "Huh! There goes Owen, thinking up something crazy again."

Well, this time he'd done more than just think. The kite was real. He'd spent weeks in the basement, cutting, glueing, carefully following his drawings, wondering if he was making dumb mistakes along the way.

It had been no use asking Mom or Dad. They only

smiled and said it looked fine. Owen wished they weren't always rushing off to work, or to one of their golf games or meetings.

And Grandpa? No help from him. Before Grandma died, he'd have been right there beside Owen, asking questions, helping, making jokes. But Grandpa was different now. It was as if a light had clicked off somewhere inside him.

The kite tugged hard against Owen's hands, and he grinned.

Neat! It swooped and soared, straining at the heavy twine. What a feeling! It seemed a living thing up there in the sky, leading Owen in swift dashes across the broad backyard.

The yard was one of the best things about living in this big old house. Backed up by a rocky hillside at the end of a dead-end street, the house had no neighbors on either side. Even the garage, which had been a barnlike stable long ago, was far off at the end of a long driveway. It was a house with lots of space around it.

Like me, Owen thought. A loner.

He shivered inside his jacket and wished he'd put on a sweater. Gloves too. The kite was pulling so hard that the twine cut into his hands. If the wind got any stronger it would lift him right off the ground, just as he had hoped.

The picture grew in his mind. There he'd be, hanging on to the kite's crossbars, floating up out of the yard, over the garage, high over the rocks beyond. Too bad the fifth grade wasn't here to see how great it—

A sudden gust of wind jerked him off his feet. He stumbled and lost his grip on the twine. The kite soared upward, wobbled, and plunged down out of sight behind the garage.

"No! Oh, don't let it be broken!" He raced to the back corner of the garage, afraid of the tangle of torn paper and broken sticks he'd find.

There was no kite there, but something else was on the ground, something that made him skid to a stop and take a hasty step backward.

A snake—a big one.

Long and scaly, it lay coiled and unmoving. How thick it was! Much bigger than the snakes that sometimes slid in and out of the rock garden near the back porch. Darker in color too, with thick overlapping scales of greenish brown.

Owen looked at the snake curiously, straining to see through an odd shifting mist that seemed to hang over the weeds and bushes in back of the garage.

Hey, it's got spikes, he realized with a start. What kind of snake has pointed spikes down its back? And a bunch of spikes at the end! What kind of snake *is* this?

The snake still had not moved. Maybe it was dead. Cautiously Owen leaned forward and peered through the thick mist for a better look.

Suddenly he felt a sharp jolt of fear.

This was not a snake at all. It was a tail, a long coiled tail that was—holy cow! It was connected to some sort of huge body!

Owen gulped. As the mist shifted, he could see a scaly leg, then another.

And claws.

And high up, something that looked like wings. Yes, dark leathery wings. For just an instant he could see them, tightly folded against a mountainous back.

A dragon!

Owen felt the breath go out of his chest as if he'd been kicked.

A *dragon!* Is it alive? How did it get here? Where did it come from? What is it going to do?

The dragon lay heavily on the ground, not moving, dim under the steamy mist that curled around its body. Owen backed away on shaky legs. Then he turned and raced toward the house, stumbling, choking on screams that scraped in his throat but wouldn't come out.

It was miles to the back door—hours of running across an endless grassy plain. He'd never make it. Long before he got to the house, he'd be swept up in those huge claws or scorched by the searing flames of dragonbreath—or both.

Just a few more steps—there! He scrambled up onto the porch, and only then dared a quick look behind him.

There was nothing in the backyard—no monstrous

beast slithering out from behind the garage, no dragon raging across the lawn roaring and breathing fire. Nothing moved, nothing that looked like a dragon. High overhead an arrow of geese shot across the sky. A pair of nuthatches scrabbled for seeds in the bird feeder. But there was no dragon.

Owen grabbed for a deep breath, then another.

Well, sure there's no dragon, he told himself shakily. What would a dragon be doing in Kings Ridge, New Jersey?

Besides, dragons aren't real. Dragons are only in fairy tales, or King Arthur stories, or little kids' picture books. Dragons are make-believe.

Not this one, Owen knew. This dragon was real.

He flung open the back door and rushed into the house.

2

THE KITCHEN SMELLED LIKE COFFEE when Owen burst in.

"There's a dragon out there!" he shouted.

His mother propped her bag of golf clubs against a chair and smiled at him. "Want some lunch, honey?" she asked as she pulled on a blue windbreaker that matched her slacks. "I'd like to see you eat something before Dad and I leave."

"There's a dragon out there!" Owen shouted again. "Dad, listen—behind the garage there's—"

"Cut it out, Owen," his father said as he rustled open the sports section of the Sunday paper. "Time you stopped thinking up silly things like this."

"I didn't think it up," Owen cried. "It's really there."

Owen's mother pushed aside the curtains and glanced out the window.

"I don't see any dragon," she said.

"You can't see it from here," Owen insisted. "It's in

back of the garage, all curled up on the ground, and—"

"There's nothing in back of the garage but weeds," Owen's father said.

"Weeds and a dragon," Owen said. "You've gotta do something. Call the police!"

Owen's father put down the paper. "Owen," he said slowly, "I know you're busy with a lot of things, but maybe your imagination wouldn't run away with you so much if you had some friends to play with."

Owen looked away. It would be great to have some friends, but there were no neighbor kids, and the other fifth graders didn't seem to like him. "Owen's weird," he'd heard someone whisper. "Smart, but . . . cripes, he has all those nutty ideas."

"Grandpa, you believe me, don't you?" he said.

Owen's grandfather shrugged.

"Oh, Grandpa, quick, you've got to do something," Owen begged.

Grandpa pulled at his gray mustache and shook his head. "Slaying dragons is a job for a younger man," he said with a faint smile. "Hugh, you'd better sharpen up your sword."

Owen's father grinned and did a mock golf swing. "Haven't got one," he said. "Do you think my new driver could handle a dragon?"

"Quit teasing. This is real," Owen said.

He felt his father's arm slide around his shoulders in a warm grasp.

"Listen, son," his father said, "I really admire that

lively imagination of yours. I always have, all the way back to the time you had that imaginary friend—what was his name?"

"Dooley," Owen answered. "But this is different."

"You bet it is," his father said. "We went along then with your invisible pal, but let's just knock off this make-believe dragon business, okay? You're old enough now to know the difference between imagination and reality."

"But—"

"Your dad's right, honey," Owen's mother said gently. "It's time to think about real things like—"

"The *dragon's* real," Owen broke in.

His mother smoothed his hair off his forehead. "Oh, Owen, why must you always try to be so . . . well, so different?"

"I don't try," Owen burst out. "I just *am*."

"And we love you the way you are," his father said. "But it's time to put that imagination of yours away for a while and concentrate on the real world."

Owen heard his grandfather sigh. "The real world's a pretty lousy place," Grandpa said.

Owen's parents exchanged looks. Owen knew that look. It meant they were worrying about Grandpa again.

"Hugh, maybe we ought to stay home today," Owen's mother said.

Owen's father shook his head as he put on his jacket. "It's the last Sunday for golf," he reminded her.

"Come on, son," he said. "Let's go outside and take a look at this dragon of yours."

"Don't get too close," Owen warned as they went down the back steps. "It's huge, and it might . . ."

His voice was lost in the beep of a horn as a car pulled up the long driveway. "Hey there, Hugh!" a voice called. "Glad you're ready. Where's Marjorie?"

Owen's father hesitated. Then he gave Owen's arm a squeeze and said, "Listen, fella, we'll check out the dragon another time, okay? Marjorie," he called as he ran back up the steps, "the Marshalls are here. Let's not keep them waiting the way we did last time."

"Owen?" It was his mother, her golf bag slung over her shoulder. "Listen, honey, there's half of last night's roast chicken in the fridge, and plenty of snacks for you and Grandpa. We'll be at the club for dinner, but if you need us . . ."

I need you now, Owen thought, but he didn't say it. As they drove off with the Marshalls, he looked nervously at the garage.

Well, at least *they're* safe from the dragon, he thought. But what about Grandpa and me?

Owen went back into the house. "Listen, Grandpa," he said, "this dragon—"

"Some other time, Owen," Grandpa said wearily. "Some other time." He put his coffee cup in the sink, turned away, and walked slowly out of the kitchen. Owen hated to see him so sad. That little flash of teasing a few minutes ago had been good, even though it hadn't helped with the dragon problem.

The dragon problem.

Could it be there wasn't really a problem at all? Everything in the kitchen seemed so snug and . . . everyday. And the backyard was still empty.

Maybe there wasn't any dragon.

Maybe he *had* made up the whole thing.

Suddenly Owen knew he had to find out.

He left the house again, this time moving slowly across the grass.

At the garage, flat against the shingles of the side wall, he inched his way to the back corner. Then he stopped and slowly stretched to peer around the edge.

The dragon was still there.

3

NOT ALL OF THE DRAGON was visible. Parts of it faded in and out of the curling screen of mist. It sprawled stomach down, its long body curved in a semicircle, its head half buried in the weeds. Its eyes were closed.

But it was alive. Every so often the great scaly body twitched in restless sleep.

Owen gulped back a sudden surge of terror. He edged back around the corner, then broke into a run, pulled his bike out of the garage and sped down the driveway.

He hated to leave Grandpa inside the house alone. Any minute the monster might wake up and go roaring toward the house spitting flames, but there was nothing else to do. He had to get help—and fast.

At the Kings Ridge police station Owen skidded to a stop, flung down his bike, and ran inside.

"Excuse me," he cried. "I need help right away!"

"Sure, what's your problem?" the desk sergeant asked as he looked up.

"There's this dragon in back of my garage!" Owen said.

The desk sergeant smiled. "Come on, kid, you've seen too many horror movies," he said. "Go home and tell your little brother your made-up stories."

"I don't have a little brother and this isn't a made-up story," Owen protested. "There's a real dragon out there, and—"

"Sure, sure," the desk sergeant said. "Just like there were real guys from outer space flying a UFO around here last spring."

"I'm telling you the truth," Owen insisted. "I don't know how it got there, but there's this great big dragon and I think it's asleep, but—"

"Okay, okay," the desk sergeant said. "Calm down, will ya?"

He got up, walked around the desk, and bent down to look into Owen's face. "Listen," he said, "are you the kid that called up about the flying saucers?"

Owen hesitated, then nodded. "I only said it *looked* like there *might* be. . ."

The desk sergeant straightened up. "How about that, Charlie?" he said to a policeman nearby. "This is the same kid, and now it's dragons."

He turned back to Owen. "Is this some kind of left-over Halloween trick?"

"No!" Owen insisted. "This dragon's real!"

The sergeant sighed. "Okay," he said, "I'm short-handed now, but I'll get a car out there when I have one to spare."

"Right away?" Owen asked.

The desk sergeant had gone back to his desk. "When I can," he said. "Now go on with you."

Owen pedaled swiftly home.

Whew! The house was still there, not burned to a charred ruin by dragonfire. Grandpa was safe too, dozing in a reclining chair with his reading glasses still on his nose.

There was no one to talk to. Only Dooley.

Upstairs in his room Owen pulled a thick notebook out of its secret hiding place. He found an empty page and began to write.

Sunday, November 12

Dear Dooley,

I haven't talked to you in a while because I was busy building my kite, but now I really need you.

Dooley, I'm scared. Nobody will believe me about this dragon, and I don't know what to do. Dragons belong in the Middle Ages, in the days of knights and castles. What is this one doing here? How did it get here? Did it travel across time and space? Can things really do that?

It's so big, Dooley. What if it wakes up hungry? What if . . .

A few minutes later Owen closed the diary and put it away. He sat back, feeling better. Good old Dooley.

You could always dump your feelings on him.

Now he had to have another look at the dragon.

Careful not to wake Grandpa, Owen let himself out of the house and ran once more to the garage. Edging his way around the back corner, he saw with relief that the dragon was still asleep. He hesitated a moment, then slowly, quietly sat down and leaned back against the shingles.

I must be nuts, he thought. Here I am sitting ten feet away from a dragon. What if it wakes up? What if it eats me?

Yet as he wrapped his arms around his legs, rested his chin on his knees, and squinted through the swirling mist, Owen realized that the pounding fear he'd felt before was gone. In its place was curiosity— and something else.

He felt sorry for the dragon.

Monstrous as it was, the dragon looked pitiful. It lay in an exhausted stupor with its eyes tightly closed, covered by great leathery lids. Small shudders shook its body from time to time as it faded in and out of the drifting mist. It looked so sadly out of place, and so alone. The back of a garage in a New Jersey suburb was no place for a dragon.

Owen stared curiously at the huge beast. When will it go away? he wondered. And how? Will it just fade away into the mist? Disappear in a big zap of flame?

Suddenly the dragon's long head twitched. Its mouth opened in a wide yawn, showing a forked tongue and rows of sharp pointed teeth. In a sudden panic Owen shrank back, but the dragon's mouth closed with a rumbling snuffle and it slept on.

The returning fear swept over Owen in a wave, and he scrambled to his feet. Gotta get out of here! he told himself. Gotta get away, fast!

The dragon shifted its weight, scattering puffs of mist. Owen caught a whiff of a wet, swampy smell that stung his nose, burned his eyes, and thickened in his throat. He choked and coughed, and ducked his head to wipe his streaming eyes on the sleeve of his jacket.

When he looked up, two huge unblinking eyes were staring straight at him.

Dark yellow eyes, they held him frozen, powerless to move.

He felt the shingles of the garage wall press sharply into his back. He tried to cry out, but although his mouth opened, no sound came. He tried to move, to wrench away from the dragon's terrible stare, but his body was as numb and stiff as if it had been turned to stone.

The dragon narrowed its eyes, raised its head, and made a rumbling sound. Then another—a rush of them. Through his numb terror Owen realized that from that huge, terrible mouth came not roars or flames, not a darting, poisonous tongue, but deep rumbling sounds that seemed like—

Like words!

The dragon was talking!

A stream of words poured from the dragon, and Owen felt the stiffness slide away from his body in a rush. His thoughts raced around in swift, tumbling circles.

It's talking to me! It's some weird language I don't know, but it's talking! That's b-better than eating! While it's talking it won't . . .

Owen pushed away the thought of those sharp teeth.

"You . . . you talk!" he said in a whispery squeak. "Hi! Uh . . . I mean, hello!"

The dragon blinked at him. The top of its head disappeared beneath wisps of mist, then swam back into view.

"Can . . . can you speak English?" Owen managed to croak.

"Englissshhhh!" the dragon said in a hissing rush. It sounded angry.

"Y-yeah, the way I talk," Owen said shakily. "Look," he went on, "s-start with my name. I am O-wen." He pointed at himself as he spoke. "O-wen," he said again slowly.

The dragon looked surprised. It raised the front of its body up on short, scaly legs and jabbed a long claw at Owen.

"O-wain?" it asked. "O-wain Glyndwr?"

Owen shrank away from the claw. "Uh, n-no," he said hoarsely. "Owen G-Griffith. Owen Thomas Griffith. Same as my grandfather, but everybody calls

23

him Tom. Everybody except me, I mean—I call him Grandpa, and . . ."

Carefully he cleared his throat. "L-listen, dragon," he went on, "do you have a name? I'm Owen. Who are you?"

The dragon glared at him.

"I am the great dragon Wyrdryn," it said proudly. Its English was perfect.

"Wow!" Owen said. "Hi, Wyrdryn! Boy, am I glad you can talk! Talk English, I mean."

"Of course I speak your cursed tongue," the dragon said. "Have not the English overrun this land for centuries?"

"Huh? Oh no, you're wrong," Owen said. "George Washington chased the English out of here a long time ago—more than two hundred years ago."

The dragon looked at Owen suspiciously.

"I know of no George Washington," he said. "I know of the noble prince Llewelyn and the great warrior Owain Glyndwr, and of their struggles to drive the English invaders forever from this land of Wales."

"Hey, this isn't Wales," Owen said. "Wales is thousands of miles away from here. I know, because that's where my grandfather's grandfather came from. It's . . ."

"You speak of thousands of miles," the dragon cut in. "What is this place if not Wales? What is its time? Its century?"

"This is America," Owen answered. "You're in Kings Ridge, New Jersey, and it's the twentieth century. But tell me how . . ."

The dragon sank back down into the swirls of mist. His eyelids drooped and he gave a great, shuddering sigh.

"'Tis worse than I thought," he said in a muffled, sad voice.

"What is? What's worse?" Owen asked.

"Gwilym's spell."

"What's a gwilymspell?"

"'Tis not a what," the dragon said. "Gwilym is a who—a wizard of mighty powers who hath banished me to this unknown ridge of kings in some strange new land of Jersey."

"A wizard!" Owen said. "You mean a magician? Wow! But how come he did that?"

"Thousands of miles," the dragon groaned. "Thousands of miles and hundreds of years from home. Oh, what a cruel punishment."

"Punishment for what?" Owen asked. "Hey, will you please tell me what this is all about? Where's this Gwilym guy? Wyrdryn? Hey, Wyrdryn, don't go to sleep. We have to talk."

There was no answer. The dragon's eyes closed wearily, and his head burrowed down into the weeds as the mist settled thickly over his body. He was deeply, heavily asleep.

Did he say banished? Owen asked himself. Some kind of punishment? What's it all about?

Owen tried to recall the dragon's words.

A wizard? Sure, back in the days of knights and castles there were lots of wizards—guys like Merlin, who did magic stuff for King Arthur.

Then it's all going to be okay, he told himself. No problem. Another shot of magic from this wizard guy and the dragon will be out of here, back in his right place and time. No problem at all.

Unless . . .

Hey, wizard, wherever you are—please, please let your magic happen soon, Owen thought urgently.

Before this dragon gets wide-awake—and hungry.

4

A S MRS. YELLEN TOOK the Monday-morning attendance and began the daily announcements, Owen squirmed in his seat.

I've got to do something about the dragon, he thought. But what?

And even if I knew what it was, how would I do it?

All through the night he had tossed in his bed, until finally at sunrise he had dressed quietly and slipped out of the house. He had found the dragon still sprawled on the ground in back of the garage, and still asleep. His scales, wet with the night's rain, caught the morning sun and glistened like polished armor.

"Wyrdryn, wake up," Owen had called softly. "Come on, wake up—please?"

With a stretch and a wide-mouthed yawn Wyrdryn had slowly come awake and blinked his yellow eyes. It seemed an effort for him to raise his head.

"Ah, 'tis you, Owen," he said wearily. "Good morrow."

"Uh. . . good morrow to you," Owen said. "Listen, we've got to talk. Tell me when this Gwilym guy is going to get you out of here."

Wyrdryn shrugged, sending trickles of water down his plated sides into oozy puddles on the ground.

"Mayhap never, if it be the king's will," he rumbled gloomily.

"What king? I thought you said it was a wizard who put a magic spell on you."

"Aye, on orders from the king."

Owen hesitated a moment, then peeled off his slicker and sat down on it. He fanned impatiently at the wisps of mist that floated between him and the dragon.

"Okay," he said. "You'd better tell me all about this king."

The dragon watched him with a flicker of curiosity. "Are all the lads in this ridge of kings as unafraid of dragons as you?" he asked.

"I *am* afraid," Owen admitted. "But you're in trouble and I guess I'm the only one around to help you. Now let's hear about the king."

"'Tis a hot temper the king has," Wyrdryn said. "When he becomes displeased with me, his anger boils like the pot of potions that steams on Gwilym's hearth. At such times he commands my punishment."

"How come he gets mad at you?" Owen wanted to know.

Wyrdryn gave a gloomy sigh. "Dragons are oft blamed for evils done by others, or for nature's tricks," he said. "Sheep stolen from a flock, a rush of rocks crashing down a mountainside and destroying a harvest—ah, 'tis easy to lay the blame on a dragon. The king rages, and orders Gwilym to cast me out of my lair to some faraway part of the kingdom. Then a few weeks pass, the king's temper cools, and he relents—and with another spell Gwilym brings me back. But this time . . ."

The dragon sighed deeply.

"What's different about this time?" Owen asked.

"This time I fear Gwilym's magic has gone amiss," Wyrdryn said in a voice filled with despair. "I am trapped here forever."

"You can't be!" Owen said quickly. "You'll go around burning things and eating people!"

There! The fear that had kept him tossing restlessly all night had finally leaped into words.

Wyrdryn slumped down even farther into the mud. "Friend Owen, I have no strength for dragonflame," he said sadly. "Behold."

He drew a breath so deep that the scales on his chest clattered. Owen shrank back, but only tiny puffs of gray smoke came floating out of the dragon's mouth.

The dragon watched the smoke mingle with the mist over his head and disappear. "You see?" he said sadly. "And as for my hunger, I eat but once a month, at the rise of the full moon, and I take care not to eat people—usually."

Owen thought of the bright moon that had lit the

sky during the night. Not full, but soon it would be—maybe in just a few more days. He shivered in spite of the thickness of his sweater.

"What *do* you eat?" Owen asked.

The dragon turned his massive head aside. "The spell lies heavily on me, Friend Owen," he mumbled. "Farewell for the nonce."

He calls me friend, Owen thought. Lucky he doesn't think I'm his enemy or I'd be gone in one gulp.

"Don't go to sleep now," he begged. "Wyrdryn, listen—you've got to get back where you belong. Tell me what to do!"

But in spite of Owen's pleas, the great yellow eyes had closed and the dragon had drifted back to sleep in the blanket of mist.

Now, as Mrs. Yellen droned on, Owen looked carefully at the calendar on the classroom wall. He'd never paid attention to the tiny crescents and circles, but they were important now, and he groaned to himself when he saw that the moon would be full on Wednesday. The day after tomorrow!

If Wyrdryn isn't gone by then, what'll I do? he wondered. How much food would it take to fill up a dragon? And what kind of food?

Owen shifted in his seat and looked around at the class. Could any of these kids help him? he wondered. Mitch Davidson, for instance—a round-faced cheerful boy who looked like he could handle just about anything. Owen wished he were friends with him.

Or even with Howie Friss, who sat two desks away. Howie was pale and skinny, and he had a way of jiggling his arms and legs when he was nervous, which was most of the time. He had steady blue eyes, though, and Owen had the feeling you could trust him not to let you down.

But it was no use. He'd never hung out with either Howie or Mitch on the playground, or done things with them after school. He couldn't just go up to one of them now and say Hey, I need help with this dragon.

And Mrs. Yellen herself? No chance, he told himself bitterly. Picture her believing there was a dragon just a few miles away from the school. Just as likely picture her teaching without worksheets or talking without the shrill capital letters she put into so many of her words.

Owen stared out the window. The bare trees still wet with rain had a glittering beauty like Wyrdryn's scales. He pulled a piece of paper out of his notebook and began drawing Wyrdryn, carefully outlining the spikes on the dragon's head, his claws, his giant body with its overlapping scales and folded wings.

It was going to be a good picture. When he got home he'd put it in his Dooley Diary, so Dooley could see what Wyrdryn looked like.

Mrs. Yellen's sharp voice drilled into his thoughts.

31

". . . and so our trip to the planetarium has UNEX-PECTEDLY been canceled. We cannot go until they have finished the repairs, and MEANWHILE it is too late to cancel the bus that has been ordered for us. We must QUICKLY plan a different trip. Suggestions, class?"

Mitch raised his hand. "How about the aquarium? Or the Bronx Zoo?"

"Naah," said Marve Parker. "That stuff's boring. Let's go to Funworld and ride the roller coaster."

Mrs. Yellen's mouth drew down in disapproval. "That is not a PROPER field trip," she said. "The purpose of a field trip is to LEARN something."

"Well, I'd like to learn how many times I can go on the roller coaster without barfing," Marve said with a grin.

Everyone laughed. Owen added another coil to the dragon's tail and tried to forget Marve existed.

Marve Parker was big. And tough. And always waiting for a chance to zing it to you if he didn't like you.

He didn't like Owen Griffith.

Owen smiled at the pleasant thought of Wyrdryn roaring flames at Marve while chasing him down the Jersey Turnpike.

Across the room Pam Lee twisted her ponytail and wiggled her tongue around the shiny wire braces on her teeth. She always did that when she was thinking. "How about the Museum of Natural History?" she said. "Let's go see the dinosaur skeletons."

"That's baby stuff," the girl next to Pam said with a sniff. "Can't we go see something better than dead dinosaurs in a museum?"

Without thinking, Owen said almost to himself, "We could go see the live dragon in my backyard."

Marve heard him. "Hey, Mrs. Yellen!" he shouted. "Owen said he's got a live dragon in his backyard!"

The class exploded into noise.

"How big is he? Where'd he come from?"

"Hey, Owen, is he green and scaly? Does he breathe fire?"

"Hoo-ee! Tell him he can come over to my house and play with Godzilla!"

"No, *my* house—I've got the Creature from the Black Lagoon!"

Marve's voice boomed above the others. "How come he hasn't eaten you, Owen? Doesn't he like SHRIMP?"

"Shut up, you guys!" Mitch yelled. "Lay off!"

Marve was out of his seat now. "Look at me!" he hooted, prancing around with his shoulders hunched and his hands curled into claws. "I'm a dragon, a great big scary dragon!" A parade of boys formed behind him, clawing the air, snorting and laughing.

"CLASS!" Mrs. Yellen shouted. "SETTLE DOWN, EVERYONE!" She banged angrily on the small humpbacked bell on her desk. "ROOM 502, I'M COUNTING! ONE—TWO—"

If she got to five, there would be spelling worksheets

33

instead of lunch-hour playground. The class settled down with a spatter of snickers and a few leftover dragon snorts. Owen bent over his notebook and wished he were invisible.

"WELL NOW," Mrs. Yellen said with a twitch of her shoulders. "Since NO ONE has had a GOOD suggestion for our field trip, I will make the choice. We will go to the Colonial Village. There are costumed guides who will demonstrate how the people of New Jersey lived long ago, and I'm SURE you will all LEARN A GREAT DEAL."

Everyone groaned.

"I'd rather go to Owen's backyard and learn about his pet dragon," Marve said with a sneering glance at Owen.

"Math books," Mrs. Yellen snapped. "Page twenty-nine—the first six homework problems on your worksheet. Howard, begin."

Homework? thought Owen. Uh-oh, here comes trouble.

It came quickly. Before Howie had finished jiggling through the first math problem, Mrs. Yellen was standing beside Owen's desk.

"Well, Owen, you seem to be VERY interested in dragons today," she said with a frown, looking at his notebook. "Where is your math homework?"

"I'm sorry," Owen mumbled. "I didn't do it, because . . ."

"Because there is a dragon in your backyard, is that

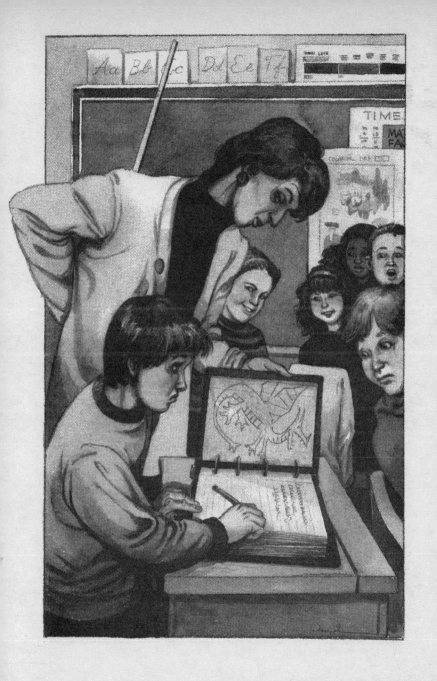

correct?" Mrs. Yellen's voice was cold, but at least she had dropped the capital letters.

Owen looked up at her cautiously. "Yes," he said. "It's been there since yesterday morning."

Owen heard Room 502 fall into silence around him.

"And is this what your dragon looks like?" She pointed to the picture he'd drawn.

Owen nodded. "Yes, he's real big, with scales all over him, and claws, and a long tail with spikes at the end. And he talks!"

Marve broke into loud snorts. "Owen knows dragon language!" he shouted. "Hey, Owen, say something in dragon!"

"He talks English," Owen said. But nobody heard him, for most of Room 502 had gone crazy again. Marve was stomping around flapping his arms, and even some of the girls were jumping up and down making dragon noises.

Mrs. Yellen's frown drew her mouth into a tight upside-down crescent. "Owen Griffith, STAND UP!" she barked. Her voice was a loud command, and the capital letters were back again.

Owen scrambled out of his seat. Room 502 went silent.

"GIVE ME THAT PICTURE!" she cried as she grabbed the paper and crumpled it. "NOW, young man, you will go IMMEDIATELY to the OFFICE! And you will tell Mr. Sanford that I will NOT put up with any more of these WILD STORIES of yours!"

"It's not a wild story," Owen cried. "It's real!"

Marve exploded into a bellow of laughter. "Yeah, real!" he hooted. "Just like the time you brought your dumb little make-believe Dooley to school!"

Mrs. Yellen whirled on Marve. "I will NOT have any more of this behavior in my classroom," she said. "You will BOTH take yourselves down to the office and DON'T COME BACK until you are ready to work like SENSIBLE fifth graders."

"Hah! She got you, Parker!" Owen heard Pam whisper as they passed her desk.

"Shut up, metalmouth," Marve snarled.

Before the door closed behind them, Owen saw Mitch flash him a sympathetic glance. At least somebody thought he was okay.

Careful to keep out of tripping range of Marve's feet, Owen made his way down the hall to the principal's office.

Mr. Sanford wasn't surprised to see either of them. He sat back from the pile of papers on his desk and smiled a tired smile.

"Well, Marvin," he said, "I can guess why you're here, but Owen—one never knows what you've been up to. What is it this time?"

Owen hesitated.

"Mr. Sanford," Marve broke in. "Remember when Owen had this make-believe friend named Dooley and he said the friend came to school and got lost on the wrong going-home bus and you had to call all the buses back because Owen wouldn't stop crying and all the kids and teachers were running around the bus yard looking for this kid that didn't exist and . . ."

Mr. Sanford sighed. "I remember Dooley," he said. "What is your point, Marvin?"

Marve turned on his politeness switch. "Well, this time, sir, it's a dragon he says he's got. And the reason we're here is because Owen made a whole bunch of trouble in class over this dragon, and . . ."

Mr. Sanford stood up. "That's enough, Marvin," he said. "Wait in the outer office, please."

As the door closed, Mr. Sanford sat down again and leaned back in his chair. "Owen," he said quietly, "at the time of the—uh, Dooley episode, you were quite a bit younger. What's going on now?"

"There's this dragon in my backyard," Owen said. "When I told the class about it, Marve started—well, they all laughed and made a lot of noise, and Mrs. Yellen got mad."

"Listen, Owen," Mr. Sanford said with a smile, "I've known you since kindergarten and you're a great kid."

I wish the other kids thought so, Owen said to himself.

"You're intelligent," Mr. Sanford went on, "and polite and imaginative and . . . well, that's the trouble, isn't it? That imagination of yours keeps getting in the way of things. Now look, I know Mrs. Yellen is a tough teacher, but do the best you can with her, okay? No funny business in class, pay attention to your work, and . . ."

"But the dragon," Owen interrupted. "I don't know what to do about it."

Mr. Sanford sighed. "Look, Owen," he said, "we all have our dragons to deal with. I have five teachers out with the flu, there's a leak in the library roof, and the president of the PTA is furious because her kid didn't get a part in the school play. Life is full of dragons of one kind or another, and we just have to handle them as best we can."

Mr. Sanford stood up and walked around to the front of his desk.

"Sometimes we can buckle on our armor and go out and slay them . . ."

Owen ducked the imaginary sword Mr. Sanford suddenly swished over his head.

"Other times it's best to retreat into the castle and pull the drawbridge up behind you. But once in a while even the bravest knight ties a white banner to his lance and works out an honorable truce with the enemy. You know what I mean?"

Owen figured it would be a mistake to say no.

"I guess so," he said.

"Good. Now while I'm taking care of our Mr. Parker, you go back to your classroom and get on with your work." He put his arm around Owen's shoulders and steered him toward the door.

"And here's some advice, just between you and me," he said in a low voice. "Try to work out a truce with that dragon in Room 502, okay?"

"Okay, Mr. Sanford," Owen said.

Grown-ups are all the same, he thought. Even if they smile at you instead of shout, they never really listen.

5

OWEN WAS SURPRISED when Pam slid into the seat across from him in the cafeteria. He usually ate by himself, hunched over a book so it would look like being alone was his own choice.

"Okay if I sit here?" Pam asked.

"I guess so," Owen mumbled. Would eating with a girl give the other kids something else to come down on him for?

Pam frowned at her sandwich. "Ugh, peanut butter," she said. "Death on braces. Hey, I sure hope Mr. Sanford blasted Parker."

"It doesn't matter," Owen said.

Pam's brown eyes flashed. "Sure it matters," she said. "Parker's a slimeball. Here comes Howie—just ask him."

Howie hesitated, then set his tray down beside Owen's. "Ask me what?" he said as he sat down.

"About that creep Parker," Pam said. "Remember all last year he called you Prissy Frissy?"

Howie's face turned red as he tore open his milk carton. "Yeah," he said. "Every year he gets on somebody's case. I guess now you're the lucky one, Owen."

"What is this, a meeting of the Victims of Marve Parker Club?"

Owen hadn't heard Mitch come up behind him. Was Mitch going to eat with him too? Great! He shoved his book aside as Mitch swung a leg over the bench and sat down.

"Why'd you go and say all that stuff about dragons this morning?" Mitch asked around a mouthful of sandwich.

"Yeah," Pam said. "That was totally weird. You should have known Parker would freak out."

Across the cafeteria Owen could see Marve Parker and a bunch of his friends pointing at him, still laughing and making dragon-claw gestures.

You did me a favor, Parker, he thought. Here are three kids from my class eating with me, almost as if they were my friends.

"It's true," he said softly. "There *is* a dragon in my backyard."

Mitch bit into a cupcake and gave Owen a chocolaty grin. "Cut it out," he said.

"You're kidding," Pam said.

"No, I'm not. It's really true."

Over his sandwich Howie stared at Owen with wide, puzzled eyes. "How *can* it be true?" he asked. "There aren't any—"

"Listen," Owen said. "Here's what happened."

42

He told them about Wyrdryn, and they listened.

Mitch licked the crumbs slowly out of the empty cupcake wrapper. Finally he looked up and grinned.

"Sure, sure," he said. "Some magic guy hundreds of years ago goes hocus-pocus—and *whammo!* This dragon goes zonking out of Wales and lands in New Jersey, right in your backyard. Come on, gimme a break!"

"This is totally nuts," Pam said. "Wales is across the whole Atlantic Ocean. And besides, Owen—dragons? Magic?"

"I know it sounds crazy," Owen answered. "But I'm telling you—yesterday this dragon came to Kings Ridge."

Howie blinked and sat back. "It must be a big lizard or something," he said. "That's what it is—a big lizard escaped from a zoo."

Owen shook his head. "No," he said firmly. "Listen, come see for yourself. Come home with me after school and I'll show you."

"Is there any poison ivy back here?" Howie asked as they followed Owen across the broad backyard.

"You're totally unreal, Howie," Pam said with a laugh. "You're on your way to meet a real live talking dragon and you're worried about poison ivy?"

"Well, I'm allergic," Howie said. "Besides, I skipped my piano lesson to come here. I could get in a lot of trouble."

"You're not the only one," Pam said. "I'm supposed

to baby-sit my little sister, and my mom'll go totally spaz if I'm late. So let's hurry it up, okay?"

"Shhh," Owen said. "Just around the corner of the garage. See?"

Mitch frowned. "See what?" he said. "There's nothing here but a lot of fog."

"Wait," Owen said. Carefully he stepped forward and peered into the mist. "Wyrdryn," he called. "Wyrdryn? Hey, I brought my fr. . . some kids to meet you."

There was silence.

"So where is he?" Mitch said.

"Asleep, I guess, under the mist. He sleeps a lot. Hey, Wyrdryn, wake up. It's me, Owen."

"Owen," Pam said. "There's no dragon here."

"Yes, there is!" Owen ran forward, flinging his arms at the mist as if to sweep it away. "Wyrdryn! Wyrdryn, where are you?"

Mitch and Howie and Pam looked at one another.

"I'm getting out of here," Howie said. "It's all mud and stuff—and it smells yucky. Come on."

Owen stepped slowly out of the mist. "He's not here," he said in a small voice. "He's gone."

"That's for sure," Pam said. "If he ever was here in the first place."

"He was! I know he was!"

Mitch looked at Owen for a minute, then shook his head. "Okay," he said cheerily as he pulled Owen away from the garage and steered him back across the

44

grass, "this was a good one, Owen, even better than Dooley. I don't know how you think up all this stuff."

"But I didn't—"

"Look what's coming!" Howie said with a moan. "My piano teacher sent the police after me!"

The squad car rolled quietly to a stop in the driveway. "One of you kids named Owen Griffith?" the driver called out the window. "Sergeant sent me to check out a complaint. Kid named Griffith reported some kind of big animal roaming around his yard."

Owen opened his mouth, but Mitch was already talking. "Must have been a mistake," he said.

"Yeah," Howie said. "There's nothing like that here."

The policeman glanced past them at the empty yard. "You sure?" he asked.

"Totally sure," Pam said. "Come on, you guys. Let's go home."

Owen stared down at the ground. They didn't even bother to say good-bye, he thought as he turned back to the house.

Upstairs in his room he dug out his Dooley Diary.

Monday, November 13

Dear Dooley,

I really messed things up this time. The dragon's gone, and I almost had some friends but they're gone too.

Now they're going to laugh at me too, along

*with all the other kids. I wish I didn't have to go
to school tomorrow.*

Or ever.

*Why did that dumb old dragon have to come
here in the first place?*

Grandpa set his cup of coffee on the table and sat down with a heavy sigh. Opposite him, Owen didn't look up.

"Cocoa too hot?" Grandpa asked after a minute.

Owen shook his head.

Grandpa stirred the coffee slowly, then laid the spoon on the saucer with a little clink. It was the only sound in the kitchen for a long time.

"Well," Grandpa said at last. "Aren't we a fine pair."

After a long silence he spoke again. "Never saw you so downhearted, Owen," he said. "That's okay for an old geezer like me who's got nothing to live for anymore, but a young boy like you?"

Owen stared into his mug of cocoa.

"I guess I'm not very good company," Grandpa said. "You and I used to have good times, didn't we?"

Owen didn't answer, but it wasn't a question anyway.

Grandpa sighed. "Yes, there were good times for all of us," he said. "Your grandmother and I had a great time together. Used to love living in the city, seeing the shows, going to the parades. Never missed a one. New York was our playground. But I'll never go back

46

to that apartment—except to pack up and move out someday."

Owen raised his head. "I miss her too, Grandpa," he said softly.

Grandpa nodded without looking up. "I know. But it's different for me," he said. "For fifty years she was my wife—and my best friend too. And now I . . ." His voice choked off and he drew his hand across his eyes.

Owen slipped out of his chair, went around the table and put his arms around his grandfather's shoulders.

"I'm your friend, Grandpa," he said.

The hug lasted a long time. At last Grandpa dried his eyes and blew his nose.

"Well now," he said with a nod. "Friends listen to each other's troubles, and it seems to me you've just had a big dose of mine. So now it's your turn. Do you want to tell me what's got you so down?"

Owen told him. And Grandpa listened.

"Well now," Grandpa said after he had heard it all. "That's quite a tale. Hold on, hold on," he added quickly. "I don't mean you made the whole thing up. What I mean is, well, it's quite an adventure, quite unusual to . . . er, meet a dragon."

"Nobody thinks I really did," Owen said unhappily. "And now the dragon's gone and I guess I ought to be glad, because he was so big and dangerous—but all I can think about is how these kids I told you about think I made it all up and I'll never be able to prove I didn't, and . . . everybody thinks I'm weird."

"Umm, that's a tough one, all right."

"Would you like to see where he was?" Owen asked after a moment.

"Well . . . okay," Grandpa said. "I guess we've sat here moping long enough. Let's go."

The mist behind the garage had thinned to wisps that were disappearing swiftly.

"Here's where I found him," Owen said, "with his head facing that way and his tail coiled up here."

"Uh. . . yes," Grandpa said. "Must have been a large fellow. Very large."

"He was humongous," Owen said. "And he had—hey, look!"

"Um? Look at what?"

"Over here! See? Scaleprints in the mud!"

"Scaleprints? Come now, Owen, I don't think—"

"And here—here's claw marks! Must have been his back claws, they're so big. Look! It's almost like a trail!"

"Owen, you shouldn't—"

"It *is* a trail! He went right through these bushes! See how they're all flattened down in places?"

"Owen, if he's . . . er, gone back to his own time and place, there would hardly be a trail left behind."

"Grandpa, follow me!"

Owen plunged through the bushes toward the rocky ravine. Behind him he could hear his grandfather calling him, but he was too excited to stop. Burrs pulled at him and fallen saplings bumped against his knees, but he thrashed on through the underbrush until . . .

"Wyrdryn! You're not gone!"

The dragon lay in a cavelike hollow between two huge rock formations. Mist floated around him as he turned his yellow eyes on Owen.

"I am not gone," he said. "I have simply moved to a proper abode."

"But this morning all you wanted to do was sleep."

"Aye, but then I found my strength beginning to return."

"But why did you come out here to these rocks?"

"Friend Owen, last night's rain was chill on my back, betokening the season of snow and icy winds. I need a lair in which I can be snug for the next few centuries. This place will serve me well."

Nearby the bushes waved and crackled. "Owen— where are you?" Owen heard his grandfather shout.

Startled, Wyrdryn raised himself up angrily on his front legs. "An enemy comes! Stand aside!"

"No!" Owen shouted. "It's not an enemy—it's my grandfather!"

Puffing, Grandpa fought free of the last clump of thorns and burrs. "Owen, where. . . Oh my!"

Wyrdryn crawled out of the hollow. Then, slowly and magnificently, he drew himself up to his full height. His scales, green on his back, yellow on his underside, gleamed in the late afternoon light. The

spines on his back shone like polished ivory, and he uncoiled his tail in steady waves. Looking down from his enormous height, the dragon unfolded his black, leathery wings until, like twin umbrellas, they spread dark shadows over Owen and his grandfather below.

"Grandpa," Owen said, "this is . . . I mean, I'd like you to meet Wyrdryn."

The dragon nodded proudly and blew two small spurts of red flame out of his nose. Then he opened his mouth in a smile that revealed the rows of sharp, pointed teeth.

"I am honored to meet you," he rumbled politely.

Owen grinned with delight. "What do you think of him, Grandpa?" he asked. "Grandpa? Are you all right?"

Wyrdryn smiled grandly and waited.

A faint bit of color came back into Grandpa's face. "H-how do you do," he finally managed to say. "It is . . . a great honor to meet . . . a dragon."

6

LATER, SITTING CROSS-LEGGED in the shelter of the rocks, Owen smiled at his grandfather. The dragon lay close by, resting after his glorious display.

"Owen, are you sure it's safe to be here?" Grandpa asked in a low voice.

"Pretty sure," Owen said. "I know he's a dragon and all that, but he's sort of friendly. Just show him you're friendly too."

Grandpa cleared his throat.

"Well now . . . er . . . Wyrdryn," he said, "you seem to be in fine shape for someone who has come all the way from another century."

The dragon stretched himself more comfortably on the floor of the cave. "I gain strength as each hour passes," he answered. "Never have I been in the grip of such weariness."

"Jet lag," Grandpa said with a nod. "And it's no wonder, considering that you've traveled three thousand miles and hundreds of years. Now suppose you tell Owen and me about your plans for returning to your proper time and place."

Wyrdryn sighed a large puff of damp gray smoke.

"I have no plans," he said. "I am at the mercy of Gwilym's spell. However, I might settle happily in this place if it is like Wales. Are there mountains and waterfalls? Peat bogs? High cliffs overlooking the crashing sea?"

"No," Owen answered slowly. "Mostly there are houses and highways and shopping malls."

"What of castles, then?" the dragon asked. "Wales is filled with castles, each with its own wizard, its company of knights, and its bard."

"What's a bard?" Owen asked curiously.

"A storyspinner," the dragon answered. "A teller of tales, a singer of songs."

"Like Gwilym?"

The dragon shook his head. "Gwilym has not the gift of story," he said. "His is the gift of magic, but because it is magic gone wrong, I am now cast adrift."

"Well, you can't stay here," Grandpa said. "We . . . er, can't have a fire-breathing dragon roaming around Kings Ridge."

Wyrdryn gave a haughty sniff. "I see you know little of the ways of dragons," he said. "Dragonflame is only for ceremonial occasions—or for destroying enemies foolish enough to attack me."

"Well then, what about food?" Grandpa went on. "Surely a dragon of your size—"

"You need not worry about that either," the dragon interrupted. "As I have told Owen, I eat only when the moon is full. That is when the Grand Procession takes place."

"Procession?"

"Each month, at the rising of the full moon," Wyrdryn said patiently, "the people come to my cave with torches flaming in the moonlight, and music, and the king himself leading an ox with bright-colored ribbons wound round its horns."

"The ox is for you . . . to eat?" Owen asked.

"Of course. It is part of the ancient agreement, you see. In exchange for the ox I promise not to prey upon other animals of the countryside for another month."

Owen gulped. "But there aren't . . . we don't have any oxen around here."

"I must have an ox," the dragon said firmly. "And now and then a princess."

"A *princess*?"

"Yes, a young lady of royal breeding, beautifully dressed and brought to me in an even grander procession. To eat, of course."

Owen felt his grandfather's hand tighten on his arm.

"Come now," the dragon said impatiently, "surely

there is a goodly supply of princesses in this ridge of kings."

Owen shook his head. "No princesses," he said.

"How can that be?" demanded the dragon.

"Well now you see, there aren't any kings or queens here—or in any part of America," Grandpa said. "We have presidents instead."

"They're sort of like kings," Owen put in. "Except that every four years we get to choose a new one."

"Ah, then bring me a cast-off president. Make it one who is sweet-tasting and juicy."

"You don't understand," Owen said. "Presidents aren't for eating. They're for making speeches and thinking about laws and taxes."

"*Yuggch*," Wyrdryn snorted. "How tough and stringy these presidents must be. Very well, I will content myself with the ox."

"That's impossible, Wyrdryn," Grandpa said. "There aren't any oxen here."

The dragon's yellow eyes glared as he sat up angrily. "Then call forth the wizard who serves this ridge of kings!" he bellowed. "Tell him to use his magic power to produce one!"

"We don't have any wizards here either," Owen said.

With a groan the dragon turned his back to them and slumped down. "No kings, no princesses, no wizards," he muttered. "I have been abandoned in an uncivilized land."

Owen's grandfather flung open the kitchen door and strode to the telephone.

"What are you going to do?" Owen asked anxiously.

"Call the police," Grandpa answered. "Or the National Guard. Get them out here fast."

"No!" Owen said. "Grandpa, listen—please. They'll go after him with guns, and think what'll happen. You heard what he said about using dragonflame against enemies who attack him. I bet he could wipe out the whole Kings Ridge police force with . . . with one breath. A troop of soldiers too. It would be awful."

Grandpa paused with his hand on the telephone. "It would be a slaughter," he agreed with a shudder. "You're right, Owen, we can't have that happen. But in two days that dragon is going to be roaring hungry, and what then? We can't just go to the supermarket and buy him an ox."

"How about if we buy him something else?" Owen said. "Hot dogs, maybe. Or burgers and French fries. Pizza."

"American fast food for a Welsh dragon?" Grandpa said doubtfully.

Suddenly his mustache twitched and he smiled. "Well, why not!" he said. "It's a fine idea, Owen! We'll stuff him so full that he won't even think about not having an ox. And then we'll have a whole month to figure out what to do about him."

Owen's eyes shone. For the first time since he had found the dragon he didn't feel as if there were a heavy stone inside him.

"We can even have a procession!" he cried. "There'll be you and me and Mom and Dad, and we'll . . ."

Grandpa shook his head. "No," he said. "I think we'd better work this out without your parents. They won't find it possible to deal with a real live dragon. No, we'll need those kids you told me about. Call them up right now. By George, we'll give that creature a procession!"

Owen looked up Mitch's number and hesitated. "What if they won't want to come?"

Grandpa touched his gray mustache and raised an eyebrow. "Tell them if they don't, they'll miss the best adventure of their lives!" he said.

After Owen finished the calls, he thought of something else.

"What about the feast?" he said. "It'll cost an awful lot."

Grandpa chuckled. "Never mind," he said. "It isn't every day I get to treat a dragon to dinner!"

"I d-don't know why I'm doing this," Howie said later as he followed Owen and his grandfather around a clump of bushes. "What if there really is a dragon?"

"There won't be," Pam grumbled. "This is totally—"

Her voice was cut off by a shout from Mitch. "Ho-lee cow! Look over there!"

Pam gave a strangled squeak.

"Hi, Wyrdryn," Owen called. "I brought some kids to meet you. This is Howie, Mitch, and Pam. Pam's not a princess," he added quickly.

Wyrdryn drew himself up and bared his sharp teeth in a smile. "I am honored to make your acquaintance," he said as he dipped his massive head in greeting.

Owen grinned at the others. "Now do you believe me?" he asked.

"I believe you, I believe you," Pam managed to croak. "My gosh, Owen!" she said in a whisper. "Is—is he tame?"

Owen hesitated. "He's a dragon," he whispered back. "Dragons are . . . what they are."

"D-does he eat people?" Howie asked in a shaky voice.

"Only princesses," Owen answered, but Howie didn't look convinced.

As they slowly drew nearer, Mitch said, "Let's find out for sure. Say, uh, Sir Dragon—do you ever eat . . . uh, just plain people? Like boys, I mean?"

Wyrdryn wrinkled his long nose with distaste. "I ate a stable boy once, when the ox was too small to satisfy me. A bony lad he was, all knees and elbows—and witless to have gone outside the castle walls at the time of my hunger. *Yaach!*"

"Would you eat any of us?" Mitch persisted.

The dragon swung his head close. As he peered sharply at them with his large yellow eyes, Howie slid behind Grandpa.

"You are friends of my friend Owen," Wyrdryn said with dignity. "It is not my nature to eat a friend."

Are they my friends? Owen wondered. It would be great if the dragon was right.

"What's all this stuff about princesses?" Pam wanted to know.

"An ancient tradition," Wyrdryn said. "All dragons crave an occasional princess to eat. A princess, you know, is trained to go calmly and nobly to her fate, should it be required of her."

"Boy, are you lucky Pam isn't a princess," Mitch said. "No way would she just stand here all calm and noble and let you eat her."

"That's for sure," Pam said. She sounded as flip as usual, but Owen saw her tongue slide nervously over her braces.

"D-do you eat any other kinds of people besides princesses?" Howie got up his courage to ask.

"Knights," the dragon answered. "But only those who would be dragon slayers. Miserable clanking fellows, they are, with their foul-tasting armor. *Pffugh!*"

"Then how come you eat them?" Howie asked.

"'Tis a fitting end for those who draw sword against me," Wyrdryn said. "But it is not pleasant to eat a knight. Too much shell and too little meat."

With a sudden clatter he settled back on his

haunches and waved them all away. "Go now, friends, for I am weary," he said. "Return at the rising of the moon two nights from now. Friend Owen, I trust there will be a Grand Procession?"

"You bet!" Owen said.

"And my hunger will be satisfied?"

Owen's friends looked uncomfortable, but Grandpa smiled.

"Friend Wyrdryn," Grandpa said with a twinkle, "never in all the centuries has a dragon had a feast like the one you are going to have!"

7

A T NOON RECESS the next day Owen pulled
the others into a tight little group at the
edge of the playground.

"Here's the plan," he said. "Grandpa's taking care of
the food for tomorrow night, and my folks are going
out early, which is lucky because it'll give us time to
fix up the ox."

Howie blinked. "What ox?"

"Owen, are you nuts?" Pam said. "How are we ever
going to get an ox?"

"He's got it all figured out," Mitch said. "We put an
ad in the Kings Ridge *Herald*: WANTED: ONE OX.
MUST BE WILLING TO BE EATEN BY DRAGON. NO EX-
PERIENCE NEEDED. Right, Owen?"

Owen grinned. "Wrong," he said. "What we do is
make a fake ox. Then tomorrow night we load it up
with food and take it out to Wyrdryn in a Grand Procession."

"How do we do all that?" Howie asked.

"Easy," Owen said. "For starters we need something on wheels, like a wagon or a supermarket cart, only bigger."

Pam ran her tongue over her braces. "How about my little sister's baby carriage?" she suggested. "It's only been sitting around in our basement since she grew out of it."

"Sounds perfect," Owen said. "Bring it to my house tomorrow after school."

Owen could hardly believe it. Instead of spending recess whacking a tetherball around all by himself the way he usually did, here he was with a bunch of friends, making plans together. And what plans!

"But a baby carriage isn't hairy," Howie was saying. "And it doesn't have horns, so how can it look like an ox?"

"How about covering the whole thing with a blanket?" Mitch said. "The one on my bed is dark brown—sort of ox color, I guess."

"Great," Owen said. "Bring it. And wait'll you hear the best part! Guess what's up in the attic at my house? It has two glass eyes, two ears, a great big nose, and antlers!"

"A stuffed moose head!" Pam shouted.

"Just about the best one you ever saw!" Owen said. "We'll hitch it to the front of the baby carriage, and—"

"Instant ox!" Mitch cried.

Howie's feet had started jiggling. "Wyrdryn's too smart to fall for anything like that," he said. "He'll know right away it isn't a real ox."

"So we tell him it's a special kind that only lives in America," Owen said. "A New Jersey moose-ox! Listen, once he smells the food, it won't matter. This morning he was thrashing his tail around and griping about how hungry he's getting. It was scary."

Howie shuddered. "Then let's start working on it. I'm not so sure he really meant all that stuff about not eating his friends."

Wednesday, November 15

Dear Dooley,

Things are great!

I wish you were real so you could be part of the procession tonight. You would like my new friends—including Wyrdryn.

I wanted to tell Mom and Dad, but Grandpa says they're not young enough or old enough to handle it. They'd flip out, he says, so we have to keep it a secret.

You should see Grandpa these days! I know he's still sad about Grandma, but he's getting to be like he used to be.

Gotta go now. There's a lot to do!

"Here's your pizza," the delivery boy said as he slid a stack of cardboard boxes onto the kitchen table. "All of 'em extra large, with mushrooms, peppers, pepperoni, and double cheese—the works. Must be some big party you're having here tonight."

Owen smiled. "Here's the money," he said. "And thanks a lot." He closed the door and turned to his friends.

"I'm glad we got pizza," he said.

"Do you really think Wyrdryn's going to like it?" Howie asked nervously.

"Sure," Mitch said. "Wouldn't you rather eat a nice gooey pizza instead of a hairy old ox? I bet hooves don't taste good at all, and a tail would get stuck in your teeth, and . . ."

"Yuck," Pam said. "That's totally gross. Help me tie these ribbons together."

"Owen, where's your grandfather?" Howie burst out. "The moon'll be out soon!" He ran to the window and looked out at the darkening sky. "What's taking him so long?"

Owen hid his own nervousness. "He told me he was going to his apartment to get something."

"Oh no!" Howie cried. "All the way to *New York*?"

"Yummm, what smells so wonderful?" Owen's mother asked as she and Owen's father came into the kitchen. "My goodness, are all those boxes filled with pizza? What in the world—"

"It's for a party," Owen said quickly.

His mother frowned. "Owen, I'm glad your friends are here, but you can't have a big party when we're not home, and we're leaving any minute. And where did you get money for all that pizza?"

"From Grandpa," Owen said. "He's . . . chairman of the food committee."

"You hear that, Marjorie? The senior citizens finally dragged him in," Owen's father said with a smile. "Isn't that great! It'll do him good to get interested in something else besides—where is he, anyway?"

"Uh, he went to New York—to the apartment," Owen said. "But he'll be back *real soon*," he added with a glance at Howie.

"Why, he hasn't set foot in the apartment since your grandmother died," Owen's father said. "Wouldn't it be fine if—"

"Hi, kids!" Grandpa said as he flung open the door. "Wait'll you see what I've got! Oh, Marjorie—and Hugh! Thought you'd both be out this evening."

"We're just about to leave for the town council supper meeting," Owen's father said. "I hear you're involved in a big pizza party at the senior center tonight. That's great. How come the kids are going too?"

Grandpa shot a puzzled look at Owen.

"The head of the food committee needs helpers," Owen said. "Right, Grandpa?"

Grandpa's eyes widened. Then he nodded. "Right," he said. "Now you two hustle along to your meeting. The kids and I have work to do."

As soon as Owen's parents drove away, Mitch asked eagerly, "Did you get the burgers?"

"Better than that," Grandpa said with a grin. "Out

66

there in the car I've got a hundred pounds of raw meat and a big pile of soup bones and a string of sausages. Where's the baby carriage?"

"Under the back porch," Pam said. "And the moose head's hitched on, and so are the pull ropes and all the ribbons except these."

"We're all set, Grandpa," Owen said. "And so is Wyrdryn."

"Yeah, you should have seen him a little while ago!" Mitch said. "Sitting up and acting like the lord of the castle. 'HO, MY FRIENDS—THE SUN SINKS LOW. IT WILL NOT BE LONG BEFORE MY FOUR-LEGGED FEAST!'"

"Cut it out," Howie begged. "Let's start loading the moose-ox, okay?"

"Okay," Owen said as he switched on the porch light. "Let's do it."

At last the moose-ox stood ready at the edge of the bushes. In the moonlight its glass eyes gleamed, and the fur on its moth-eaten ears stuck up in silvery tufts. Pam put down her load of pizza boxes to straighten the bright plastic flowers draped around its neck and smooth the ribbons looped over its antlers.

"Doesn't it look great!" she whispered. "Mr. Griffith, you're super to have brought a fur coat! I love the way the sleeves hang down near the front wheels almost like legs!"

"Grandpa, are you sure it's okay to use Grandma's

fur coat like this?" Owen asked.

Grandpa smiled. "It's old," he said. "I was going to buy her a new one, but I never had the chance. I think your grandmother would be very pleased to have something of hers in this Grand Procession." He pulled his tweed cap down over his forehead and cleared his throat. "Well now, is everybody ready?"

"Final check," Owen said. "Torches?"

Howie and Pam turned on their flashlights.

"Music? That's me." He snapped on the cassette player hooked to his belt. "Okay—all systems go. Rope bearers, pull! Grandpa, push! Dragon, here we come!"

Loud rock music boomed as the procession moved through the dark shadows. Owen and Mitch pulled ropes tied to the carriage frame, while Grandpa pushed against the handle and tried not to trip on the swaying tail of sausages. In back of the moose-ox, Pam and Howie balanced armloads of pizza boxes, while their flashlights gave off wobbly beams of light.

"Whew, this is hard work," Mitch shouted over the noise of the music.

"And how," Owen shouted back. The cassette player bumped against his leg and the rope bit into his hands, but when he looked behind him, he liked the way the moose head bobbed as the carriage moved over the bumpy ground.

"We're almost there," he shouted to the others.

"I hope so," Howie shouted back. "This stuff is

heavy—and there's grease dripping through the boxes."

At last the procession reached Wyrdryn's rocky cave.

"Procession, halt!" Owen shouted.

He dropped the rope and stepped forward. "Hail, mighty Wyrdryn!" he called. "The full moon rises and we have come in Grand Procession with your feast!"

Wyrdryn was waiting. He sat majestically on his haunches, his long tail arranged in artful coils in front of him, his front legs folded on his chest. His scales glittered magnificently in the moonlight. When he caught sight of Owen, he sent orange and red flames curling around his massive head like a brilliant wreath.

Then he dipped his head in a lordly nod and blew a shower of sparks.

"Welcome," he said graciously. "I accept the tribute you bring in honor of the ancient agreement between humans and dragon, and once again I pledge—What *is* that terrible noise?"

Owen snapped off the cassette player. "You said the procession had to have music."

"Music, yes, but not yowling," the dragon said with a scowl. "We will dispense with the music—and also with the ceremonial speeches. Lead forth the ox!"

"Yes, Mighty Dragon. The feast will begin with an ancient New Jersey custom—the eating of something so delicious that—"

"Hurry," the dragon snapped. His tongue flickered in and out of his mouth hungrily. "Hunger howls in my stomach."

"Okay, okay," Owen said hastily. "Comrades, step forward," he called.

Swiftly Howie and Pam piled the pizza boxes on the ground in front of Wyrdryn, then ran back, wiping their greasy hands on their jeans.

As Wyrdryn looked on suspiciously, Owen flipped open one of the boxes. "Doesn't this smell good?" he said.

The dragon put his long snout down and sniffed. "What is this oozy cartwheel called?"

"Pizza," Owen answered.

"WHAT?" Wyrdryn roared angrily. "Peasants warm their huts with peat! They foul the countryside with its smoke! You would have me eat something made of PEAT?"

"No, no," Owen said quickly. "It isn't made of peat. That's just its name—peet-zah. It's good, honest it is."

He scooped the pizza out of its box and held it out with both hands. "Here, have a taste."

"My stomach rumbles for its ox," the dragon complained, but he opened his huge mouth. Hastily Owen tossed the pizza in and jerked his hands away just as the great jaws snapped down.

As Wyrdryn slurped and chomped, Owen looked nervously back at the others in the shadows. Finally he asked, "Isn't that delicious?"

Wyrdryn's tongue darted in and out, scraping

71

strands of cheese off the scales around his mouth.

"It has not the flavor of ox," he said at last, "but it is good, in a new and strange way. Have you brought me other dishes native to my new land?"

"Indeed we have, O Mighty Dragon," Owen said. "Comrades, bring forth the . . . uh, beast."

Wyrdryn's bony eye ridges rose as Grandpa and Mitch trundled the moose-ox forward.

"What is this creature?" he asked.

"O Splendid One," Grandpa said in his most dignified manner, "we are proud to present to you this rare and unusual New Jersey moose-ox. It is the only one of its kind."

"You'll love it," Mitch said. "Wait till you taste its tail."

Wyrdryn stared at the moose head. He poked a claw at its nose and flipped one of the furry ears forward and backward.

"Hey, you guys, let's go, okay?" Howie said.

"Okay," Owen said. He bowed to the dragon. "Mighty Dragon, we leave you to enjoy your feast. Remember the ancient agreement—you won't eat anything else around Kings Ridge, will you?"

Wyrdryn appeared too busy to answer. Squinting curiously, he had coiled his long tail around the baby carriage and was drawing it closer.

Owen and the others scrambled away from the rocks. Behind them there was silence.

After a few minutes Owen turned. "Look!" he whispered.

By the light of the round November moon they saw the dragon peel the fur coat off the baby carriage and peer inside. His eyes gleamed. With a swoop of a front claw he reached inside and speared a large chunk of meat. With another he snapped off the string of sausages. Then he stuffed everything into his mouth.

"It worked!" Mitch said.

"Yeah," Owen said happily. "Now we can relax for a whole month."

Howie took one last look at the dragon and shivered as he zipped his jacket higher.

"Let's hope," he said.

8

THERE WAS TOO MUCH NOISE on the school bus for talking, but Owen didn't care. He had a lot to think about. For once, all of it was good.

A lot had changed in just a couple of days. He had friends—three of them! He was sure of it now. And Grandpa was more like he used to be.

And the problem of feeding the dragon had been solved.

He sat back happily and pretended to look out the window. Over the chatter of the fifth grade and Mrs. Yellen's repeated shouts for order, he heard his private White House hot line ring. It was the president again.

"I'm sorry, Mr. President," he heard himself say into the telephone, "but it's no use. The dragon doesn't want to move to the cave you've built for him at the White House. He wants to stay with me and my friends and Grandpa.

"Yes, I know he's an extremely valuable endangered species, but we really take very good care of him. And you don't have to worry a bit about him being dangerous. He's really quite friendly.

"Oh, he asked me to tell you he is very happy with the ox your special government agency sends him every month, but maybe once in a while you could include some pizza with it. Double cheese.

"What's that? You want Wyrdryn and me to fly down to Washington when the Prince of Wales comes for a state visit? Sure, we'll be glad to. And after that . . ."

The bus jolted to a stop and Mrs. Yellen's voice cut into Owen's thoughts.

"Now, class, when you get off the bus you will be in a DIFFERENT WORLD," she said. "I want you to notice how EVERYTHING looks EXACTLY as it did in colonial America. Be sure to look CAREFULLY at the costumes worn by the people here. EVERYTHING has been made by hand and is ABSOLUTELY AUTHENTIC."

Owen looked around as he walked away from the school bus. Men in knee pants and women in long dresses strolled along narrow streets of small houses and shops. Through an open door he could see a woman tending an iron kettle at a large stone hearth. Another, wearing a white ruffled cap, sat busy at a spinning wheel.

The class straggled after Mrs. Yellen as she picked her way over the paving stones. "Now STAY TOGETHER, class," she called. "First we'll go to the one-room schoolhouse. Follow me."

"Some field trip," Marve grumbled. "We came all this way to go to another school."

Mitch caught Owen's sleeve. "Did Wyrdryn say anything to you this morning about how great the feast was?" he asked in a low voice.

"I didn't have time to go out and see him this morning," Owen answered. "I was so late getting up I missed the bus, and Mom had to drive me to school."

"Owen, Mitchell—come along," Mrs. Yellen's voice cut in. "Don't lag behind."

"Yeah, Owen," Marve mocked. "Quit DRAGGIN'— get it?"

Owen turned away from Marve's dragon imitation. He wouldn't make his crummy jokes if he saw Wyrdryn, he thought.

"My, that was INTERESTING," Mrs. Yellen said when they came out of the schoolhouse. "Next we will go to the smithy. And on the way, I want you to watch for some of the villagers making preparations for next week's Thanksgiving feast. Observe CAREFULLY, because someday soon you'll be doing worksheets on today's visit."

Some of the class groaned, but not Owen. Even Mrs. Yellen's worksheets couldn't spoil the way he felt now that Wyrdryn had been fed.

"Hey, this is neat!" Mitch cried as he pointed to the flames roaring in the forge. The blacksmith's hammer beat a rhythmic clang, and sparks flew as a red-hot horseshoe took shape on the anvil.

At the cooper's shop they watched men making

wooden barrels. In several of the houses women sat weaving at large looms, and at the print shop men in inky aprons were setting type one letter at a time and lifting pages of a newspaper from a large printing press.

"And now for a SPECIAL TREAT," Mrs. Yellen said as she led the way toward the end of the street where a barn stood behind a rail fence. "We are going to the mill, to see grain ACTUALLY being ground into flour. That VERY flour will later be made into bread for the Thanksgiving feast."

"This is fun, isn't it?" Howie said as they walked along.

"Yeah," Owen agreed. But it would be a lot more exciting, he thought, if it were a village in Wyrdryn's century.

As he looked at the neat wooden houses and shops, he saw instead huts with thatched roofs. Some of them lay near fields of grain and cabbages, but others huddled close to the walls of a great stone castle.

The cobblestone street disappeared and turned into a muddy, rutted cart trail. Knights on tall horses clattered along, past townspeople in rough tunics celebrating not Thanksgiving, but Fair Day. Peddlers sold bright ribbons and bears danced and jugglers tossed colorful balls into the air. And Wyrdryn, perched on a rocky crag near his cave high above the village, watched it all with a dragonly smile.

"You mean there's to be NO DEMONSTRATION?" Owen heard Mrs. Yellen say.

The class had come to the mill and had gathered around two thick stone wheels that lay one on top of the other, in a heavy wooden frame.

"I'm sorry," said a man wearing brown homespun knee breeches. "All I can do today is explain to your class in words how the grain is ground. In early colonial days farmers would bring their grain here to the miller—that's who I am. I would pour it gradually onto the bottom stone. Then, while this top stone moves slowly around on the bottom one, the grain would be ground into flour."

"How can you move a stone so big and heavy?" someone asked.

"Oh, I can't," the miller answered. "But it's no problem for a twelve-hundred-pound ox."

"You've got a real ox?" Pam burst out.

The miller frowned. "Yes and no," he answered. "Last night somebody broke into the barn, and old Muff got out. So we can't do any grinding until we find the big fellow and bring him back."

Owen's stomach twisted into a knot.

"Wh-where do you think old Muff might be?" he asked uneasily.

"Oh, wandering around in the fields someplace, I guess," the miller said. "We've had people out searching, but there's no trace of him so far."

"Why in the WORLD would anyone break into a BARN?" Mrs. Yellen said indignantly.

"Hard to figure," the miller said. "But they sure did

a job on those doors."

Owen turned to look. The barn's wide wooden doors leaned open at awkward angles, partly torn away from their iron hinges. Splinters of wood curled down in thick strips, and a heavy wooden bar lay on the ground, snapped in half. Inside, the barn was empty except for a few bales of straw.

Owen flicked a glance at his friends. Pam's face had gone pale, and Howie was biting his upper lip hard. Even Mitch looked sick.

"Wow, look at those doors," someone said. "Looks like somebody went at 'em with a hatchet."

Or with claws, Owen thought.

In spite of the cold November air he began to sweat.

On the way home Owen and his friends huddled together on the backseat of the bus.

"Oh my gosh," Howie wailed softly. "He was expecting twelve hundred pounds of ox. What we gave him must have seemed like just a little snack, and . . ."

"And after he chomped it down he went off to get a real meal," Mitch said.

"How would he know there was an ox there?" Pam asked. "*We* didn't."

Owen tried to make his stomach stop churning. "Dragons have a super sense of smell," he said. "I read it in a book."

"What are we going to do now?" Pam wanted to know.

Nobody had any ideas.

"Hey, maybe we don't have to do anything," Mitch said. "Maybe old Muff just wandered away someplace. They might even be bringing him back home right now."

It was just like Mitch to try and be cheerful, but it didn't work this time. The sick feeling in Owen's stomach wouldn't go away.

When the bus got back to school, Owen turned to his friends. "You better come over to my house," he said. "We've got to tell Grandpa, and then . . ."

At the cave Owen and the others looked at the sleeping dragon in dismay. Bones were heaped around Wyrdryn, who seemed to be smiling in his sleep. Only an occasional hiccup broke his deep, contented breathing.

"Boy, he's never going to want to leave here now," Mitch said in a low voice. "Look at the terrific deal he's got—pizza and stuff from us and then a little hunting trip of his own."

Pam turned her face away. "How could he do such an awful thing?" she said.

"I guess it didn't seem awful to him," Owen said. "He was only doing what dragons do."

"You're right," Grandpa said. "We shouldn't assume that just because he can talk like a human being, he's going to act like one."

"We should have given him more food," Mitch said.

The dragon stirred in his sleep and flicked his tail. A cluster of ox bones went rattling over the rocky ground.

"It wouldn't have made any difference," Howie said as he jiggled nervously. "Dragons go around eating anything they want to. Next time it might be people."

"Wyrdryn wouldn't do that," Owen said, but he didn't feel as sure as he sounded.

"Next month we'll feed him more," Mitch said. "Just in case."

"No!" Howie said. "We've got to get him out of here before next month. Way before, like *now*."

Grandpa put his arm around Owen. "Howie's right," he said. "This dragon is too big a problem for four kids and an old man. It's time to notify the authorities."

Owen was quiet as they left the cave, but his thoughts raced. A zoo, he thought. Zoo people won't come after Wyrdryn with guns, the way police would. Once they took him away, though, would they keep him scrunched up in a cage? Wyrdryn would hate that. He might even try to burn down the zoo with dragonflame.

Maybe some scientific research people, then. No, they'd keep him in a cage too, and after they finished counting all his teeth and scales, they'd probably cut him up to find out what dragons are like inside.

There didn't seem to be any good solution.

Owen made his steps match Grandpa's as they came out of the brush and started across the grassy yard. "Grandpa, what are we going to do?" he said. "We can't just . . . *OOF!*"

A sudden wind whipped around the corner of the garage and slammed into them all, sending them reeling against one another and knocking them to the ground. The gust stung their eyes and whipped Pam's ponytail around her face.

"What's happening?" Howie yelled.

With a loud thump a whirling cloud bounced off the back wall of the garage, spun up into the air, then dropped to the ground and slowly settled into a thick mist.

There was something familiar about that mist. Owen raised his head and squinted at the billowing white cloud.

"There's something all crumpled up on the ground," Pam whispered hoarsely as she crawled over to him. "Wh-what is it?"

"I don't know. It looks like a bundle of old cloth," Owen whispered back. "And a lot of white fur, all tangled up. No, not fur—it's hair."

And suddenly, even before he heard the faint groan that rose out of the mist, Owen knew.

"It's the wizard!" he cried happily. "Gwilym's here!"

9

"HELP HIM UP!" Owen cried. "Oh boy, Gwilym, are we glad to see you!" He tugged at the still form that lay on the ground.

The bundle of cloth groaned again. A hand clutched at Owen, and a faint voice croaked out a question in a strange-sounding language.

Owen felt happy all over. "You've got to talk English, Gwilym," he said with a laugh. "I know you can, just like Wyrdryn."

"Wyrdryn!" The wizard tried to pull himself up, but collapsed again in a heap. Owen tugged at him again.

"Slow down, Owen," Grandpa said. "The poor man's exhausted."

"But we've got to take him to Wyrdryn!" Owen cried.

"Wyrdryn . . . be . . . in . . . this . . . place?" The words were muffled by a shaggy white tangle that

Owen guessed was a beard.

Grandpa bent over the wizard. "Yes, yes, he's here," he said soothingly. "But sound asleep, so there's no hurry to—Oh, my good fellow, what you need is a bath! And a long rest. Owen, all of you—help me get him into the house."

Mitch and Howie edged their way into the mist. Lurching and tripping over the wizard, they managed to drag him clear of the mist. Pam darted into the swirling fog and grabbed a lumpy leather pouch that lay on the ground.

"*Oof,*" she said as she struggled to pick it up. "This guy sure doesn't travel light."

Together they helped the wizard stumble slowly across the backyard. In the kitchen at last, they lowered him into a chair, where he slumped over the table, head down on his arms, breathing heavily.

His white hair and beard were matted and tangled. He wore a dark-red tunic made of a heavy tapestrylike cloth and soft, shapeless leather boots that were tied around his ankles with thongs.

"I thought wizards wore shiny clothes with moons and stars all over them," Howie whispered. "And tall pointed hats."

"Only in cartoons and comic books, I guess," Owen whispered back. "This one's a *real* wizard." He smiled to himself. Real wizards, real dragons—how could you be sure anymore what was really real?

The leather pouch made soft clunking noises as Pam heaved it onto the table.

"What do you suppose is in this duffel bag?" she said.

"Stuff for magic spells, I hope," Owen said. "Gwilym . . . uh, Sir Wizard, are you okay?"

The wizard slowly raised his head and straightened up. With a deep, shuddering sigh he leaned back in the chair and focused dark brown eyes on Owen and the others.

"I . . . have . . . found . . . Wyrdryn?" he asked in a weak voice.

"You sure have," Owen said.

"And just in time too," Howie added. "You've got to get him out of here fast."

Grandpa cleared his throat. "Well now," he said, "we . . . er. . . bid you welcome, Gwilym. Here's some good hot coffee."

The wizard looked quizzically at the steaming mug, then curled his hands around it and drank. "Umm," he said, then sighed again. He looked curiously around the kitchen. When he spoke, his voice was stronger.

"What is this place? In what world do I find myself?"

"This is Kings Ridge, New Jersey," Owen said. "You're in America, and it's the twentieth century—almost the twenty-first. And these are my friends and my grandfather. We've been trying to take care of your dragon. Things haven't been going too well, but . . ."

He smiled at the wizard. "But now that you're here . . ."

The wizard stood up shakily.

"I must go to Wyrdryn," he said. "I must return us both to our rightful time and place."

"Oh please, not right away," Owen said.

Grandpa put his arm on the wizard's sleeve. "We'll take you to Wyrdryn," he said, "but you'll find him in a deep sleep. He . . . er, had an ox for dinner last night."

The wizard nodded. "Then indeed he will sleep until the morrow," he said.

"And you need sleep too," Grandpa said. "You can have the bed next to mine in the guest room, and I'll lend you a pair of pajamas."

"I do not understand this talk," the wizard said, "but indeed I am weary." He sank back down in the chair and looked around.

"And I do not understand this room of shining doors and strange boxes," he said.

Owen followed the wizard's glance around the bright kitchen with its Formica cabinets, gleaming stove and refrigerator, microwave oven, food processor, coffee machine. That's not all you won't understand, he thought with a smile. Wait'll you see toilets and television!

Thursday, November 16

Dear Dooley,
  Our problems are over—the wizard's here!
He's a lot like Grandpa, but he's got long hair
and big bushy eyebrows, and when he looks at you

it's like he knows all about you. I think I like him.

Tomorrow he's going to make the spell that will take him and Wyrdryn home through hundreds of years.

It's kind of scary. I never met a real wizard before. But I never met a real dragon before either.

Isn't it great? Everything's going to be okay now.

(I hope.)

"Boy, Owen, I bet your folks went totally spaz when they came home from work and met a wizard!" Pam said the next morning in school.

"They didn't get to meet him," Owen said. "He was in bed asleep when they got home, and he missed dinner and everything. He wasn't even up when they left for work this morning."

"Didn't they think that was kind of weird?" Howie asked.

Owen shrugged. "Grandpa told them he was an old friend who had flown in from far away and had a lot of jet lag to sleep off."

"That's for sure," Pam said with a laugh. "Hundreds of years' worth!"

"Besides," Owen said, "they're real glad Grandpa has a visitor. They've been worried about how lonely he is."

"I can hardly wait to see Gwilym and Wyrdryn split for Wales," Mitch said. "I wonder what the spell will be like."

"Probably just a lot of weird words," Pam said. "Abracadabra or something. And then—*poof!*—they're both totally gone."

"I wonder if he'll wave a magic wand," Owen said.

"I don't care what he does," Howie said, "as long as he and Wyrdryn get out of here. When it gets to be Thanksgiving, I want to give thanks for no more dragon."

After school they raced to Owen's house, where they found Gwilym in the kitchen, drinking coffee with Grandpa.

"Wow! You look great!" Pam said.

"I am not long from my slumber," the wizard replied with a pleased smile. "And I have had a bit of American magic."

"Otherwise known as a shower and a shampoo," Grandpa said with a twinkle.

The wizard ran a hand over his soft white beard. "Such wonders there are in this dwelling!" he said. "A sleeping nest of soft cloth. Floors covered with thick tapestries. Boxes that cook without fire and cool without snow. And think you—a whole room in which water flows from many springs and a whirlpool appears by pressing a handle!"

Grandpa smiled. "My friend Gwilym has seen the marvels of modern living," he said. "And tasted some of them too."

"Bagels!" the wizard said with enthusiasm. "And cheese as white and soft as a cloud! Pastry baked by the Danes! Butter churned from peanuts, whatever they are—and best of all, this strange black brew that fills me with the strength of a warrior knight!"

"Totally awesome!" Pam said.

Howie was jiggling from one foot to the other. "Can we please get the show on the road?" he said impatiently.

Grandpa stood up. "It's time, Gwilym," he said.

"You are right," the wizard said with a sigh. "I must dally no more. Let me now face Wyrdryn and beg forgiveness for the dreadful mistake that sent him here. Then we will return to our rightful home."

"I wish you didn't have to go so soon," Owen said. "Wyrdryn and I—well, we were sort of getting to be friends."

The wizard smiled but shook his head. "Too long has my search for Wyrdryn kept me from my duties," he said. "The king's impatience will have no end."

He picked up his leather sack.

"What have you got in there?" Pam asked curiously.

"Materials for my most powerful spells," the wizard said as he patted the pouch proudly. "Now take me to the dragon."

At the cave, Wyrdryn was now wide-awake. He sat lazily picking his teeth with a long rib bone, looking over his shoulder to admire the way his tail scales shone in the late afternoon sun.

Grandpa caught the wizard's arm and pulled him behind a rock. "Better let us go first," he said quietly.

"You stay here till we signal."

"Don't say anything about the ox," Owen whispered to the others as they picked their way around bones and bits of oxhide.

Howie gulped. "That won't be hard," he muttered.

"Well now, Wyrdryn," Grandpa called as he stepped forward. "I see you're finally awake."

The dragon rippled his tail, coiled it into a gleaming spiral, and tilted his head in a dignified nod. "I had a small afterdinner nap," he said with a smile.

"We have a surprise for you," Mitch said.

"Not food, I hope," Wyrdryn said with a bored yawn. "I cannot hold another morsel—although a small taste of peet-zah might be nice."

"No, it's not anything to eat," Owen said. "It's a person—someone you know."

The dragon raised a scaly eyebrow. "I know no one in this ridge of kings but you," he said as he looked from one to the other.

Gwilym could wait no longer. He burst out from behind the rock, waving his arms. "Wyrdryn—I have found you!" he cried.

The dragon reared up in surprise. "YOU!" he roared. The spikes on his back quivered, and a hot red flame shot from his nostrils as he glared angrily at Gwilym.

"May your liver shrivel into dust!" he cried. "May your nose grow until it wraps itself around your neck!"

"Ungrateful wretch!" the wizard shouted back. "I

have searched the centuries for you, and you greet me with curses!"

"How should I greet the maker of my misery?" Wyrdryn raged. "'Twas your careless spellmaking that cast me out of my home and flung me through time to this kingless ridge!"

"'Tis a misery you brought upon yourself," Gwilym snapped. "To steal the king's gold and then deny your guilt!"

"Never did I touch a single coin!" Wyrdryn roared. "May your skin turn blue if you believe such a monstrous lie. May the soles of your feet turn to iron, and may . . ."

The dragon stopped. Great round tears swam in his yellow eyes. "Ohhhh, Gwilym!" he moaned. "I thought you would never come to my rescue! Let us go hoooome!"

He dropped to the ground with a clatter, and a torrent of Welsh words burst from him. Gwilym answered soothingly, and soon wizard and dragon were murmuring together in their strange, mouth-filling language.

Owen tugged at his grandfather's sleeve. "Is everything okay now?" he asked.

Grandpa wiped his eyes on his handkerchief and nodded. "I imagine they're telling each other how glad they are to be together again," he said in a husky voice.

After a while Gwilym straightened his tunic, smoothed his beard, and turned to the others.

"I thought . . . never to see him again," he said.

Pam's eyes were shining, but Howie was jiggling nervously. "Is the reunion over yet?" he asked.

The dragon looked down at them all and swept his front paws about in the air graciously. "Ho, my friends," he said. "It is time to say farewell."

"Farewell," Howie said quickly.

"Good-bye, Wyrdryn," Pam said. "It's been nice . . . I mean interesting to know you."

"Gee, Owen," Mitch muttered, "should we shake hands—I mean paws?"

Owen kicked at a pebble and said nothing.

He felt the dragon's eyes on him and had to look up.

"I . . . I'm sorry to see you go," he said finally.

The dragon blinked down at him, then bent close. Gently he stroked Owen's shoulder with the smooth curve of one claw, and Owen saw that puddles of tears had begun to well up again in his yellow eyes.

"Never will I forget you," Wyrdryn said softly. "You are a lad who understands loneliness."

"I won't forget you either, Wyrdryn," Owen managed to say.

Grandpa cleared his throat. "Well now," he said. "I think we're all ready. Gwilym, the . . . er, stage is yours."

Gwilym nodded. He reached for his leather pouch and opened it. With both hands, he pulled out a black iron pot the size of a baseball and placed it carefully

on a flat rock near Wyrdryn. Owen saw that the pot stood on three short legs shaped like dragon feet, with tiny scales cleverly molded into the iron claws.

In front of the pot Gwilym arranged small, bulging packets made of coarsely woven cloth, and next to them a tiny metal bottle. Then he dug once more into the pouch and drew out a thin yellow stick the length of a ruler. Like a conductor calling an orchestra to attention, Gwilym tapped the stick on the rim of the pot.

Then, muttering a low chant over the cloth packets as he opened them, he poured their bright-colored powders into the iron pot. With a flourish and a louder chant, he dipped in his wand and stirred. Puffs of red, blue, and green dust rose from the pot.

Howie sneezed.

Poor Howie, Owen thought. He's even allergic to magic.

Still chanting, the wizard opened the metal bottle. Out of it drifted a twist of gray smoke that grew longer as, snakelike, it wrapped itself around the outside of the pot, then curled down inside. There was a rumbling sound and the pot began to shake. Gwilym's chanting grew louder. He swung his yellow wand in the air and pointed it first at Wyrdryn, then at himself. Quickly the dragon waved at Owen and the others, then closed his eyes tightly and clenched his claws.

"Good-bye, Wyrdryn!" Owen shouted as he waved back.

"So long!" Pam called.

"Happy landings!" Mitch yelled.

Howie waved between sneezes.

"Bon voyage!" Grandpa called. "And to you too, Gwilym!"

The rumble grew into loud, thunderous booms. A huge puff of rainbow-colored smoke leaped out of the pot and swirled around the dragon and the wizard, growing larger and larger until it covered them completely. Flashes of dazzling light darted about, bouncing off the rocks in sizzling sparks.

"Ow!" Owen cried. He flung his arms over his head and turned away with eyes squeezed shut against the blazing lights and the thunderous noise.

Then there was silence.

The lights vanished.

The smoke cleared.

Owen slowly lowered his arms and opened his eyes.

The dragon and the wizard were still there.

10

OWEN TURNED UP THE COLLAR of his jacket against the cold.

It feels as if we've been here for hours, he thought as he hunched down against the wall of rocks and squinted at the sunset.

Nearby, the wizard was still trying spells. This time he was holding a dark-blue ball in his hands, bending over it and chanting in a low singsong voice.

Howie crawled over to Owen. "What do you suppose this one is?" he whispered.

Owen looked at the tiny lights glowing faintly inside the sphere. They looked like stars. And those little balls moving around that one star—they must be planets.

"I think it's a model of the solar system," he whispered back. "I bet he's trying to line up space and time in some magical way."

Howie blew on his hands to warm them. "I sure hope it works," he muttered.

As the chanting grew louder and the sun in the middle of the ball brightened, Owen held his breath. But the light flickered out and the ball went dark.

Gwilym flung it aside with an exasperated grunt.

"Never before have I known so many of my spells to fail," he said.

"How about trying the magic wand again?" Pam suggested. "Maybe it'll work this time."

Gwilym gave the wand a halfhearted flick, then shook his head.

"Nothing works," he said. "I have tried everything—my whole stock of spells and charms, all my powders, every trick of magic I have ever known. 'Tis no use."

"I knew it," Howie groaned.

"I guess," Grandpa said slowly, "magic from your time just doesn't work in ours."

Wyrdryn gave a snort and blew a puff of gray smoke out of his nostrils. "'Tis not the time," he said. "'Tis the place. A land without a wizard of its own is not open to magic."

"So what do we do now?" Mitch asked. "If Gwilym's magic won't work in New Jersey, where does that leave us?"

"It leaves *you* snug in this kingless ridge where you belong," the dragon went on sadly, "but Gwilym and I are cut off forever from our home, a land where the very air crackles with magic."

"But you can't stay here," Howie said. "Right, Owen?"

Owen didn't answer. He was rolling an idea around in his mind.

"Gwilym, listen," he said slowly, "do you think your magic would work if you and Wyrdryn were in Wales instead of in New Jersey? I mean, if you could get back there to make your spell, would it take you back to your own time?"

The wizard frowned thoughtfully. "'Tis likely there are many in Wales who even now believe in the ancient powers of magic," he said. "Yes, I doubt it not. Were we there today, my magic would leap from my wand and fling us back through the years."

"That's it then!" Owen cried. "All you have to do is fly to Wales!"

"Get real, Owen," Mitch cut in. "Dragons aren't allowed on airplanes."

"Who's talking airplanes?" Owen said as he pointed to the huge wings folded against the dragon's back.

"You mean fly with his own wings?" Howie said. "But it's thousands of miles—across a whole ocean!"

"So what?" Owen said. "Birds fly across oceans, and so do butterflies. It would be easy—right, Wyrdryn?"

"Right, Friend Owen!" the dragon answered as he pulled himself up proudly. "Certain it is that I can stay aloft for hours, swooping and soaring, riding the wind currents over the seas, and . . ."

"How about you, Gwilym?" Owen asked. "Could you make it across the ocean on Wyrdryn's back?"

The wizard hesitated. "'Tis a hard way to travel, but . . . yes, I think it could be done," he said.

"Well then, let's do it!" Grandpa said. "All aboard, Gwilym!"

The wizard stuffed the wand and the dark-blue ball into his pouch and stepped into the middle of the scaly paw Wyrdryn stretched down to him. He moved carefully, holding the bottom of his robe away from the sharp claws.

Wyrdryn lifted the wizard up to his shoulder, tilted the cup of claws, and opened it so Gwilym could step out.

"Wow, look at him go!" Mitch said admiringly as Gwilym climbed over a hill of shoulder scales to the ridge of spikes on the dragon's back.

"Ready for takeoff?" Grandpa called.

Gwilym nodded. He settled himself between two spikes and leaned forward. "Open your wings, Wyrdryn," he commanded.

Wyrdryn's wings rippled slightly, quivered, then slowly unfurled until they arched over his body like twin black sails.

"Holy cow!" Mitch said. "Look how big they are!"

"Totally awesome!" Pam breathed.

The dragon began to move his giant wings up and down, slowly at first, then faster and faster. With each stroke a powerful wind gusted down on Owen and the others.

But Wyrdryn remained on the ground.

"Where's all that swooping and soaring he bragged about?" Howie said. "Maybe he can't fly after all."

Grandpa pulled at his mustache. "Nonsense," he said. "All dragons can fly. He's just . . . out of practice."

"Give it another try, Wyrdryn," Owen called up to the dragon. "Go out there in the field and get a good running start."

"A fine idea, Friend Owen," the dragon said. He moved away from the rocks, flexed his massive back legs, then leaned forward and began to run. As he streaked along, his wings flowed up and down with smooth, powerful strokes. Pebbles scudded across the ground, bushes snapped, and trees bent.

Owen struggled to stay on his feet against the rushing wind that flung showers of dust and leaves at him and nearly toppled him over.

Faster and faster Wyrdryn ran. Harder and harder his wings beat. Louder and louder Owen and the others cheered him on, their shouts lost in the thunder of the dragon's feet and the shrill whistle of the wind.

Wyrdryn thrust out his long neck and strained for a leap into the air.

Mitch grabbed Owen's arm. "Liftoff!" he yelled. "Yaaaay!"

"Nooooo!" Howie yelled back. "Look!"

The dragon's body jerked as if held down by an invisible chain. He toppled over, claws and tail thrashing wildly. As he skidded to a scale-rattling stop, the wizard lost his grip and fell off.

Owen and the others ran through the clouds of dust. "Wyrdryn, are you okay?" Owen shouted.

"Gwilym, are you hurt?"

The wizard stood up and brushed the dust from his robe. "I much prefer magic as a way to travel," he muttered.

Wyrdryn shook himself, and his scales smoothed down with a clatter. As his great black wings settled back into their tight folds, he swung his head angrily down toward the wizard.

"I have lost the gift of dragonflight," he snapped. "Is this too your doing?"

Gwilym wrung his hands. "Truly I meant it not," he said. "So hot was the king's anger that he demanded of me a banishment spell more powerful than any I had ever made before. Oh, Wyrdryn, never did I dream that my magic would go so far beyond its usual powers. Not only have you been flung through time and space, but . . . alas, you have been bound to the earth as well!"

"He's grounded!" Howie cried. "Oh my gosh, what are we going to do now?"

For a long moment everyone was silent. Then Owen said, "Uh, Gwilym, your spells don't work here, but . . . well, how about an unspell? Is there any way you could . . . undo the grounding?"

The wizard stroked his beard. "'Tis a clever thought, lad," he said, "but the undoing of spells is not one of my specialties. However," he quickly added when he saw Owen's look of disappointment, "let me see." He rummaged in his pouch and pulled out a thick leather-covered book decorated with strange pictures and symbols.

"Look at that!" Mitch muttered. "A user's manual for magic!"

The wizard turned the parchment pages carefully.

"Hmm," he said. "'Caring for Your Crystal Ball.' I haven't looked at this section since I was a young apprentice. Let me see now. . . 'Foretelling the Future.' 'Recipes for Potions.' 'Enchantments.'"

"That sounds like the right part," Owen said. "What does it say?"

"'Enchantments of People'—that would be knights, princes, peasants. 'Of Animals'—mostly toads and frogs."

"Isn't there anything about dragons?" Pam asked.

The wizard turned a page. "Here it is—'Dragons.' 'Dragon Bites: How to Cure.' 'Dragon Fights: How to Stop.' 'Dragon Flights'—No, it says nothing that would be of help to us."

"Keep looking," Owen begged.

The wizard bent over the book and studied it. "Ummm," he mumbled to himself. "Ah, here we are: 'Spells: How to Do.' 'Spells: How to Undo.' Ah, here—I had forgotten. 'Failed Spells: How to Correct.' Hmm, umm . . ."

"What does it say?" Howie burst out.

"It tells of strange and wonderful magic, lad, but there is nothing about overcoming the grounding of dragons."

Owen looked over the wizard's shoulder. On a page covered with strange symbols were pictures of people floating in air. "What's this part about?" he said.

"'Levitation,'" the wizard read. "Um, yes, quite so—but for our needs useless. It cannot be done. To levitate a dragon would require powerful magic, and as we know . . ."

"Forget it," Howie said gloomily. "Wyrdryn's grounded and we're stuck."

"*He's* the one that's stuck," Pam said. "Oh Wyrdryn, if we could just unstick you from the ground, I bet you'd fly as good as you used to."

Gwilym glanced up at the huge wings folded on the dragon's back. "You are correct, young lass," he said. "If only he could be lifted free, so that no part of him touches the earth, then indeed he would be able to fly."

"Then all we have to do," Owen said slowly, "is get him up in the air."

"No problem," Mitch said. "Anybody got a sky-hook?"

"Let's be serious about this," Grandpa said. "How about a construction crane?"

They explained to the wizard what a construction crane was.

"'Twould not do," he said as he shook his head. "The crane itself would be touching the ground, or 'twould be mounted on some building that rests on the ground."

"It wouldn't work anyway," Owen said. "There would be so many chains and steel cables, he wouldn't be able to move his wings. We've got to think of something else."

"Hot air balloons?" Pam said. "One of those blimps that float around over football games?"

"A zillion Happy Birthday balloons filled with helium?" Mitch said. He gave Owen a friendly poke. "Hey, Owen, you used to talk about building a kite big enough to lift you off the ground. Here's your chance to make one that would lift a dragon!"

Pam tossed her ponytail. "Get real," she said. "Wyrdryn's too heavy for any old kite."

"Come on, Owen," Howie pleaded. "You're always the one with the ideas. What are we going to do?"

Owen dug his hands deep into his pockets and squinted thoughtfully up at Wyrdryn.

"I don't know," he said. "But there's got to be a way."

"Let me serve you some lasagna, Mr. Gwilym," Owen's mother said.

The wizard frowned at the mound of pasta, cheese, and tomato sauce on his plate, and Owen held his breath.

Uh-oh, he thought. Back in the days of knights and castles people didn't have food like this. They didn't have forks either. They ate with their fingers or speared chunks of meat with sharp pointed knives.

Across the table Grandpa picked up his fork and signaled silently to Gwilym. The wizard watched carefully, then poked his own fork into the lasagna.

Owen let out a long breath. Not too much food slipped off before it reached Gwilym's mouth.

After a few bites the wizard smiled. "'Tis wondrous good," he said. "And to have turned from a frozen block into this steaming dish in so short a time . . . 'tis magic!"

Owen's mother beamed. "Microwave magic," she said. "Would you like another helping?"

"Better save room for the pie, Gwilym," Grandpa said with a smile.

"I hope 'tis songbird pie," the wizard said. "'Tis my favorite."

Owen's mother looked puzzled, then smiled. "I like your sense of humor, Mr. Gwilym," she said. "It's apple pie—with ice cream."

"This is great," Owen's dad said. "It's the first time my father has invited anyone here. You must be a special old friend."

Old friend? Owen thought. More like ancient! And special, for sure!

Of course Gwilym didn't look much like a wizard now, in a blue turtleneck sweater and gray flannel pants borrowed from Grandpa. And of course his magic doesn't work, Owen reminded himself. Still, he's a wizard just the same, and it's wonderful.

Except for the problem of the dragon.

"Are you here on business?" Owen's father asked.

The wizard hesitated and Grandpa stepped in. "The export business," he said. "He's trying to arrange the shipment of . . . er, some rare and antique goods."

"It's a shame your luggage got lost," Owen's mother said. "I hope the airline will find it."

Grandpa helped himself to more salad. "We'll go shopping for clothes tomorrow," he said with a smile.

Grandpa sure has his appetite back, Owen thought. Some of his old pep too. If only Wyrdryn and Gwilym could stay . . .

He took a piece of garlic bread and sighed.

"Say, there was some excitement out at the Colonial Village," Owen's father said. "Weren't you out there with your class, Owen?"

"Y-yes," Owen said cautiously.

"Did you know their ox disappeared? I heard on the news that it was found—well, anyway parts of it—in a gully near the Village. Bones, bits of hide—lots of blood."

"Oh Hugh," Owen's mother broke in with a shudder. "What an awful thing to talk about at the dinner table. Owen, honey, you've gone so pale!"

"Might be there's some kind of dangerous animal on the loose," Owen's father went on. He leaned over to Owen with a smile. "You know, it reminds me of your wild story about that dinosaur in the backyard." He turned to Gwilym. "Our son has a very lively imagination."

Owen shot a look at Grandpa, but Grandpa frowned and shook his head.

"The police are out with search parties," Owen's father went on. "They're asking anyone with information to call them."

The police? That sergeant will remember, Owen realized. He'll send his men back here, and they'll go poking around, and this time they'll find Wyrdryn.

Owen could see the police creeping up on Wyrdryn, aiming their guns at him, shooting. The bullets bounced off the dragon's scales, but Wyrdryn turned with a roar of rage. Red-hot dragonflame blasted forth. The huge sharp claws ripped and slashed. As Owen and the others watched helplessly, the furious dragon flung charred, bloody bodies against the rocks.

One man escaped, gasped into his walkie-talkie for help, and army tanks came rolling in, tearing up the lawn, crushing the garage, firing shells at Wyrdryn, and . . .

Dishes clattered as Owen's mother got up to clear the table. "I don't want to hear any more about search parties for dreadful creatures," she said. With a pleasant smile she turned to Gwilym. "We all enjoy your company so much," she said. "I do hope you can stay at least through Thanksgiving."

Owen blinked. Thanksgiving?

He sat upright in his chair. What if . . . ?

No, he told himself, it's a crazy idea.

And it's complicated. And risky.

But we have to do something, he told himself. Maybe this is it. And if it works . . .

It was a big if.

11

Saturday, November 18

Dear Dooley,

What have I got us all into?

If the plan doesn't work and Wyrdryn is captured, or killed—

I don't even want to think about it.

But what if it does work? Then Wyrdryn will be gone.

Mr. Sanford said there are three ways to deal with dragons. You fight them or hide from them or make a truce with them. He didn't say anything about getting to be friends with them.

Or about how you deal with missing them.

It hadn't been easy to get the others to agree to the plan.

"We could never do that!" Howie had gasped.

Grandpa had pulled at his mustache for a long time.

"It's an interesting idea," he'd finally said.

"It's perfect!" Owen said. "And nobody will even notice him."

"Not see a creature of my size? How can that be?" the dragon asked in a puzzled way.

"Oh, they'll see you all right," Owen said, "but they won't especially *notice* you."

"The plan has many dangers," the wizard pointed out. "Should any part of it fail, I fear for Wyrdryn."

"Well, we can't just let him sit around here waiting for the police to find him," Mitch said. "Either he flies or he dies."

Pam flicked her tongue over her braces. "It's a totally awesome plan, Owen," she said. "But it's so complicated."

"New York City in the middle of the night!" Howie wailed. "My mother will never let me."

Finally Owen had turned to the dragon. "Wyrdryn," he'd said quietly, "what do you think about the plan?"

"Much of it I do not understand," the dragon answered, "but I trust you, Friend Owen. I am willing to put my fate in your hands."

"How about you, Gwilym?" Owen asked.

The wizard hesitated, then drew himself up. "I also," he said.

"It's crazy," Howie insisted. "Too many things can go wrong."

There was silence for a moment. Then Howie

looked over at Owen and stopped jiggling. "Okay, count me in," he said.

"Me too," Pam said.

Mitch thrust both thumbs up with a grin, then slung an arm around Howie's thin shoulders. "Don't worry," he said. "This'll turn out to be the best Thanksgiving you've ever had."

"One thing's for sure," Owen added. "It'll be a Thanksgiving you'll never forget!"

A few days later Owen and the others went over all the parts of the plan. The dragon sat in front of his cave and listened intently.

"Mitch—you and Howie and Pam will drive to Hoboken with Grandpa," Owen said. "Gwilym and Wyrdryn and I will meet you there."

"How are you going to get Wyrdryn there without anybody spotting him?" Pam asked.

"If we're lucky it'll be a real dark night," Owen said.

Howie shuddered.

Grandpa unfolded a large map. "What troubles me," he said, "is that once you get away from the hills and rocks around Kings Ridge, there's not much back country anymore. It's all filled in with houses and towns and shopping centers."

"And look at all the roads to cross," Pam said as she peered at the map. "Even the turnpike."

"Hey, he could just zoom right down the pike," Mitch said. "Do you suppose there's a toll for dragons?" It was like Mitch to try to be funny at a time like this.

"I have it all figured out," Owen said. "We take the jogging trail out of Kings Ridge—nobody's ever on it at night. Then down the small roads till we get close to Paterson. And from there—" He looked up at the others. "We take the Passaic River."

Pam squinted at the map. "There's no road there," she said. "How can you go along beside the river?"

"Not beside the river," Owen said. "In it."

Howie's blue eyes grew wide. "You mean *swim*?" he said. "At *night*? In *November*?"

Owen shook his head. "All Wyrdryn has to do is wade," he said. "Gwilym and I would be so high up on his back that I bet we wouldn't even get our feet wet."

"No," Grandpa said firmly. "It's much too dangerous."

"Owen, you're crazy," Howie said. "It'll be cold. And wet. And yucky."

The dragon's eyes gleamed. "'Twould be like splashing in the bogs at home," he said. "I can hardly wait!"

"The water won't be deep close to the shore," Owen went on, "and nobody would see us, and . . ."

"It's out of the question. I won't permit it," Grandpa said.

"Grandpa, it's the only way," Owen pleaded. "Wyrdryn will keep us safe, won't you Wyrdryn?"

The dragon pulled himself up proudly. "You can

rely on me to do so," he said.

"Look, Grandpa, it's an easy route," Owen said. "Down the river to Newark Bay, then right around the tip of the bay and up to Hoboken. It'll be a cinch."

Grandpa stroked his mustache. "Well now," he said slowly, "I suppose if you were to stay away from the midstream channel . . ."

"You bet we would!" Owen said. "Even in the bay we'll stay close to the shore, and . . ." He grabbed the wizard's hand. "Gwilym, we can do it, can't we?"

The wizard nodded. "'Twill take courage," he said, "but it can be done."

Tuesday night, November 21

Dear Dooley,

    Everything's all set for tomorrow night. I guess it's good to be so busy that most of the time you forget about being nervous. I've been over at Mitch's house a lot, and Howie's too, getting all our stuff ready, and . . .

"Owen? May I come in?" It was Grandpa, standing in the doorway wearing a bright-red sport jacket with shiny brass buttons.

"How do I look?" he asked with a smile.

Owen shoved aside his Dooley Diary. "Neat-o!" he said.

"I've checked everything out and it looks okay," Grandpa said as he sat down on Owen's bed. "There are falls in the river, but you'll enter the river below them. It's all factories and empty lots, and nothing will be lit up at night, so . . ." Grandpa reached for Owen's hand.

"Owen, are you sure you want to do this?" he said.

"It's the only thing we *can* do," Owen answered. "Gwilym could fly back to Wales on a plane, but what about Wyrdryn? We've got to help him."

"Any creature that big and powerful ought to be able to fend for himself," Grandpa said with a flash of anger.

Owen looked into Grandpa's worried eyes. "Sure he's big and powerful," he said, "but he's helpless too. Grandpa, he needs us."

Grandpa sighed. He patted Owen's hand and stood up. "Better get some rest," he said. "Tomorrow night will be a . . . long one."

Owen tossed in his bed for a long time. He'd gone over the plan so many times, it seemed to be wearing grooves in his brain.

Everything's going to be okay, he told himself. Wyrdryn knows the part he has to play, Grandpa's going to handle the grown-ups, Mitch and the others have kept it all a secret. Gwilym's sure he can manage the flight across the ocean on Wyrdryn's back. So what is there to stew about? What could go wrong?

Plenty.

He punched his pillow and flopped onto his stomach. As he drifted into sleep he remembered that he hadn't finished the letter to Dooley.

Oh well, it didn't matter. Telling things to Dooley didn't seem so important anymore.

In the faint moonlight Owen could just make out the wizard's face.

"Gwilym, have you got the map?" he whispered as they waited beside the jogging trail.

The wizard patted the pocket of his windbreaker and nodded.

"And the sandwiches?"

"In my pouch," Gwilym said. "Along with my robe and the memories you and your grandfather gave me to take back."

"Souvenirs," Owen corrected. "I hope you really like them."

"I like them indeed. See? Even now under this sweater with the neck of a turtle I am wearing the T-shirt with 'I Love New Jersey' emblazoned on it."

"It looks great on you," Owen said. "Do you think the king will like the one you're taking back for him?"

"He is sure to," the wizard said. "And I cannot wait to show him the set of colorful writing sticks and the knife that folds into its own handle. Most wondrous, though, is this tube of light." He smiled with pleasure as he swept the flashlight beam over the darkness at the edge of the jogging path.

"Don't waste the batteries," Owen warned. "Nobody at the castle will have replacements. Are you sure you have the postcards and snapshots?"

Gwilym smiled again. "They are the most precious treasures of all. Think what the king will say when I show him pictures of places and people far in the future!"

"I bet he'll have a hard time believing you," Owen said, and smiled to himself. He knew a lot about not being believed.

Trees beside the jogging path rustled and the dragon appeared, pushing aside branches that scraped against his scaly chest.

"Ho, friends," he said. "I am here."

"Great," Owen said. "You didn't have any trouble getting here, did you?" he asked anxiously.

"No, but a few dogs and cats may never forget this night," the dragon answered. "What of your parents, Friend Owen?" he went on. "Did they not think it strange that you and Gwilym went off together in the night?"

"Nope, because we didn't just go off," Owen said. "We drove away in Grandpa's car with the others, and then Grandpa dropped us off here. Everybody thinks we're all on our way to Grandpa's apartment in New York, to stay overnight so we can take Gwilym to the parade tomorrow before he flies home. And that's the truth, sort of."

"'Tis not exactly a lie," the wizard said. "Ah, 'twas hard to say good-bye to your parents, Owen," he went on. "They have been kind hosts to me this past week."

118

"They like you," Owen said. "I heard Mom tell Dad you have Old World charm. Listen, we better get moving. Grandpa and the others will be waiting for us in Hoboken. Ready, Wyrdryn?"

"Ready, Friend Owen," the dragon said. "Shall you be first?"

"Sure." Owen hitched up his jeans and took a deep breath. They'd practiced several times back at the dragon's cave, but it was still a scary feeling. Carefully he stepped into the cup of claws that the dragon stretched down to him.

"Okay," he said as he sat down. "Fourth floor, please!" I'm beginning to sound like Mitch, he thought.

With a jolt the cup of claws lifted him off the ground and sped him upward. The overlapping scales of the dragon's long legs and massive body whizzed past in fast-changing patterns.

He landed against the dragon's shoulder with a bump and climbed out between the claws. Carefully he pressed the toes of his sneakers against the leathery scales and crawled forward over Wyrdryn's shoulder onto his back, inching toward the nearest spike.

There—he reached it! Thick and smooth, it was almost as tall as he was. He hooked an arm around it and pulled himself up to his feet. It took a moment to get a steady footing.

"Are you all right, lad?" Gwilym called up to him.

"Fine," Owen called back as he clung to the spike.

"Just give me a minute to make room for you."

Steady now, he told himself. He made his way slowly and carefully to the next spike, then the next, and the one beyond that, concentrating on keeping his footing as he moved along. Just a few more to go. Down the row of spikes he could see the hollow where Wyrdryn's wings grew out of his back. Another minute—and another long stretch—and he'd be safely settled in it.

There! He swung himself around the last spike and eased down until he was sitting on the leathery black skin, cradled as if in a deep saddle. With his legs straddling the spike in front of him and both hands holding on to it, he leaned over the side and peered down at the wizard.

"Okay," he called. "And be careful—some of the scales are slippery."

Before long Gwilym was sitting beside him in the wing hollow. The wizard unfolded a map, propped it against the spike in front of him, and snapped on his flashlight. "We are ready, Wyrdryn," he said. "Do you remember the route?"

The dragon twisted his head around and nodded.

"I have learned it well," he said. "Along this trail of jogs, then onto the back roads."

"Right," Owen cut in. "And stay away from anything lit up, like a gas station or an all-night shopping center. It won't be far to the river."

The river! Now that they were really on their way

120

the thought of the dark, cold water made him shiver.

Okay, then he wouldn't think about it. He'd concentrate on what he could see from this perch high on the dragon's back.

"Hey, Gwilym, look over there," he said. "That string of lights is Main Street. Be sure to tell the king how Kings Ridge looks all lit up at night."

Gwilym's eyes flashed with excitement. "Ah, 'tis an astonishment how the night is banished," he said. "And even by day this is a wondrous place. Such sights as your grandfather showed me this week! An indoor marketplace bigger than a jousting field, and filled with food enough to supply a whole city under siege! And a palace where people sit in rows and eat the white fluff of corn while they watch images of people chasing each other in the shining wagons you call cars. Truly, Owen, you live in a place of wonders."

"I think your place sounds pretty neat too," Owen said. "All those castles and knights and banners and trumpets. And magic."

And no yelling teachers with boring worksheets, he thought. And no bullies like Marve Parker.

"There's my school!" he said to Gwilym. "And there's the building where Mom has her office—right over there!"

Shielded by trees, Wyrdryn moved smoothly and steadily on past the houses of Kings Ridge.

"There's Mitch's house!" Owen called out. "And Pam's! And there's where Marve Parker lives."

The dragon skidded to a stop. "Indeed?" he said. "Many times have I heard your friends talk of the harm he causes you. Let us pay him a visit."

"No, Wyrdryn, we can't stop—there isn't time!" Owen said.

But Wyrdryn had already left the jogging trail and was striding across the dark lawn. "There is always time to deal with the enemy of a friend," he said firmly.

Light streamed from the Parkers' living-room windows, but Owen could see that Marve wasn't sitting in front of the television with the rest of the family.

"He must be upstairs in his room," he said. "He's always bragging about having his own TV."

Wyrdryn crept around the side of the house. He pointed toward the light from a window under the eaves. "Ah," he said quietly. "Is that the knave in there?"

Owen leaned forward to look. "That's him," he said. "But listen, don't hurt him or wreck his house, okay?"

Wyrdryn nodded. With the tip of one claw he raised the window.

"Marrr-vinnnn Parrr-kerrr," he called softly.

"Huh?" Marve looked up. "HUH?!"

A chair scraped and a table crashed to the floor as Marve leaped to his feet and flung himself back against the opposite wall.

Wyrdryn poked his long snout farther into the

room. His yellow eyes gleamed.

"I underrrstand you do not belieeeve in drrrragons," he growled. "Mussst I eat you to prove I exissst?" Small orange flames flickered inside his mouth as he bared his teeth in a wide and terrifying smile. Then his eyes shot forth a gleam of dragon-stare.

Owen leaned forward. It was great to see Marve frozen against the wall, his eyes bulging with terror and silent screams stuck in his wide-open mouth.

With a swift movement Wyrdryn slipped back from the window into the shadows of the trees.

An instant later they heard Marve scream as he went pounding down the stairs.

"A DRAGON!" he shrieked. "THERE'S A DRAGON OUT THERE!"

The front door burst open and outdoor lights lit up the lawn. Owen saw Marve dash out onto the porch, then cower behind his parents and his sister.

"Marvin, you're imagining things," Mrs. Parker said. "There's nothing at all out here."

Marve stared fearfully into the darkness. "Th-there is too!" he blubbered. "It's Owen's d-dragon! He came to get me! He had great big teeth and fire in his mouth, and . . ."

"That does it," Marve's father said angrily. "Helen, I told you this boy watches too many horror movies. Young man, I'm taking that TV set away from you right now."

"Nooooo!" Marve wailed.

"Serves you right, creep," Marve's sister said.

As Wyrdryn moved quietly away through the darkness, the wizard chuckled.

"Well done, noble dragon," he said.

"Gee, Wyrdryn . . . thanks!" Owen said.

They were getting close to Paterson. The trees had thinned and the land had flattened out. Housing developments and office complexes rose out of the night.

"Soon there will be no places to hide," the wizard said. "'Tis time to enter the river."

Cautiously the dragon crept toward the darkened factory buildings and warehouses at the water's edge. Owen looked at the glittering black water and gulped.

It's not so big, he told himself. Not nearly as wide as the Hudson, and I bet it's not very deep either.

Deep enough, another part of him answered. And just as wet. And it did look so cold. Owen shivered.

The wizard reached out a calm hand.

"'Tis likely our toes will not even touch the stream, lad," he said.

Owen knew Gwilym was right, but . . .

He swallowed hard and managed a nod.

"Okay," he said. "Let's go."

Wyrdryn crept carefully forward. Then, below the falls, in the shadow of a bridge, he slipped into the river.

12

THE RIVER GREW DEEPER, but Wyrdryn had no trouble keeping the upper part of his body above the water. Back legs bent in a crouch and neck stretched out low over the water, he waded steadily, using his tail for balance. As Owen looked over the dragon's side at the river below him, he felt as if he were skimming along in a boat.

Onshore there were brightly lit streets and open areas, but the stream remained in shadow as they passed.

It's easier than I thought, Owen told himself as they slid noiselessly under another bridge.

When the river opened into Newark Bay, he could see long piers jutting into the water, their lights reflecting off the black water in shiny streaks.

"It's awfully bright here," he whispered to Gwilym.

"'Tis true," Gwilym whispered back. "But we dare not go out farther, for there the water deepens beyond Wyrdryn's measure."

Owen hunched his shoulders under his jacket. I

wish we were out of here, he thought.

As they passed a freighter lying at anchor, Owen heard men talking. He looked up and saw two sailors standing at the rail. From the high deck their voices floated out over the water.

"Hey—what's that?" one of them said. "Look!"

"At what?" the other answered. "I don't see anything."

"Right out there! A great big head . . . it's a sea serpent!"

Wyrdryn crouched lower in the water and dipped his head until it barely skimmed the surface as other voices joined the shouting.

"Come on, this is Newark Bay, not Loch Ness!" Owen heard someone say with a laugh.

"Hey, Mack, you've been at sea too long," another voice said. "Too many night watches and not enough shore leave."

"Yeah? Well, there's something out there with a long neck and a long tail and I say it's gotta be a sea serpent."

"Okay, let's get some lights on it and call the captain."

Spotlights beamed onto the water from the high deck of the ship. Bells clanged and sailors crowded to the rail, jostling and pointing.

"Down!" Wyrdryn ordered.

Owen and the wizard flung themselves flat as the dragon slid his head and long neck under water. Beneath the folds of Wyrdryn's dark wings, Owen could hear the water lapping close. He strained to hear what was happening on the ship.

"There it is!" yelled a sailor. "I see it!"

Wyrdryn sank even lower until only the ridge of his back was above water. Trickles of water began to seep under the edges of his wings.

"Quiet down, men," Owen heard a firm voice say. "Look there, Mack. Your sea serpent is only a big tree trunk drifting downriver. If it's still in the shipping lanes tomorrow, the Coast Guard will get it out."

"Aye aye, sir," Mack answered. "Sorry, sir." The voices grew fainter and the spotlights snapped off, but not until they had left the bay did Wyrdryn lift his head out of the water.

The water poured off the dragon's head and neck as Owen and the wizard crawled out of their hiding place. Owen felt damp and cold, but safe again, as they made their way up the Hackensack River.

"We're almost there," he said as he peered at the dark shore. "And it's just like Grandpa said. Nothing but factories and parking lots."

A few minutes later, after he had picked his way around drainpipes and large chunks of concrete, the dragon climbed out of the water. Water slid off his scales in glittering sheets and dripped into huge puddles all around him. Owen shivered inside his damp clothes, and the wizard sneezed.

Wyrdryn turned his head. "You are cold, my friends?" he asked. "'Tis an easy thing to remedy."

He opened his mouth and blew a gentle, steady blast of heated air. It felt wonderful.

Like the world's biggest hair drier, Owen thought. He could smile again, now that he was dry and warm.

A little later Wyrdryn crept slowly down the dark streets into the outskirts of Hoboken, past factories and warehouses that loomed out of the darkness on all sides. At last he slid under a viaduct and crouched in the shadows.

"This is where we're supposed to meet them," Owen said. "I wonder where they are." He let go of the spike, slid down Wyrdryn's scaly sides to the ground, and peered out of the shadows. Far down the street, in front of a brightly lit warehouse, a crowd of people swarmed around long flatbed trucks pulled up at loading platforms.

"Is it time?" Gwilym asked. "What says the clock on your arm?"

Owen looked at his watch. "We're right on time," he said, "but I don't see them any—There they are!"

"Owen—Gwilym! You made it!" Grandpa said as he grabbed Owen in a tight hug.

Pam and Mitch ran up, eyes shining with excitement. Behind them Howie looked excited too.

"Any trouble on the way?" Grandpa asked.

Owen and the wizard looked at each other. "Nothing important," Owen said. "It was a great cruise!"

"Here's your backpack, Owen," Mitch said. "And now that we're all here how about getting started on the sandwiches?"

Grandpa shook his head. "Not till you're safely on your way to the city," he said. "Now everyone wait here. I'll give you the signal when it's time to move. Here I go." He zipped up his windbreaker and walked briskly out of the shadows, clutching a clipboard.

Owen could see that at the warehouse everything was carefully organized. Loading crews were carrying heavy bundles of bright rubber and plastic to the trucks, while people with clipboards called out numbers and motioned the huge flatbeds closer.

Wyrdryn's eyes gleamed and his tail began to twitch with excitement.

A crew of men heaved a massive load onto a truck, covered the load with a canvas tarpaulin, and lashed the corners down with ropes. They waved the driver on to make room for the next truck.

"Look—there's Grandpa," Owen said. "He's got one."

"Pull it up over here," they heard Grandpa shout to the driver of a huge flatbed. "Over near this viaduct—easy, easy, a little bit closer, that's right. Good."

The driver leaned out of the cab window. "Thought I was supposed to take this rig right up to the loading dock," he said.

"They're not ready for you yet," Grandpa said. "There's plenty of time. Come on, let's go get a cup of coffee."

"Sounds good," the driver said, and turned off the engine. While he climbed down from the cab, Grandpa looked back toward the shadows of the viaduct and swung his arm in a beckoning circle.

"Now?" Wyrdryn asked in a whisper.

"Now!"

Quickly the dragon slid out of the shadows, hoisted himself up onto the truckbed, and stretched himself out flat on his stomach.

"Pull your tail in and curl it up around you," Owen said. "Be careful your claws don't drag off the side. Okay, you guys. Let's do the tarp."

As the wizard and the others ran to the truck, Owen climbed up beside Wyrdryn and began unrolling the tarpaulin. Mitch and Pam scrambled up beside him, tugging at the thick ropes and tossing them over the side to Howie and Gwilym.

"Pull hard," Owen called as the heavy canvas unfolded. "Spread this end over his tail and tie it down."

"It's stuck someplace," Howie called back. "I think it's caught in his back claws. Wiggle your foot, Wyrdryn. Okay—there, I've got it."

Swiftly they worked until half of the dragon was covered with canvas.

"Get his head covered—hurry up!" Howie called as he looked nervously over his shoulder. "Uh-oh—too late! Owen—they're coming back! What'll we do?"

"Get up here fast!" Owen whispered. "Everybody under the tarp. Wyrdryn, shut your eyes and don't even breathe!"

Howie and the wizard scrambled up and dove under the canvas with the others as Grandpa and the driver came back to the truck.

"Hey, it's loaded already," the driver said with surprise. "How come?"

"Well now, they must have sent a loading crew over here," Grandpa said. "Things get more efficient every year."

The driver peered up at Wyrdryn. "What is this thing, some kind of lizard?" he said. "I thought I was supposed to take Superman."

Grandpa looked at his clipboard. "Change in plans," he said. "This is your load all right. Let's get the rest of the tarp over it. Go around to the other side and see if everything's fastened, will you?"

"Everybody okay in there?" Grandpa whispered. "Got enough air?"

Owen squeezed past Wyrdryn's front leg and peered down at Grandpa. "Everything's fine," he whispered back.

Grandpa gave him a quick smile, slid the canvas over the rest of Wyrdryn, and tied the rope loosely. "All set," he called to the driver. "Let's go."

"You coming along?" the driver said in a surprised voice.

"Yeah, I'm on the unloading crew too," Grandpa said. "Let's get going. There's still a whole night's work to do."

The doors of the cab slammed shut and the engine started with a roar. As the truck moved slowly down the street Owen snuggled down comfortably next to the others in the curve of Wyrdryn's shoulder.

"Here we go!" he whispered excitedly. "Isn't this great?"

"It sure is," Mitch said. "Now let's eat!"

13

I T WAS WARM UNDER the tarpaulin, and dark. They huddled together against Wyrdryn's huge body as the truck swayed and bumped along the streets.

Pam swung her flashlight up at the folds of canvas draped over Wyrdryn's spikes. "It's just like being in a tent," she said.

"Careful with that flashlight," Owen warned. "The light might get out at the edges, and we don't want anybody to think there's something weird in here."

"What's weird about a truckload of dragon?" Mitch asked with a grin.

Pam clicked the flashlight off, and they all settled down in the darkness.

"Let's go over everything again," Howie said. "Just in case something goes wrong."

"Knock it off," Mitch cut in. "Nothing's going to go wrong." He punched Owen's backpack into a pillow. "Wake me up when we get there."

How can anybody sleep now? Owen thought. He

pressed the button on his watch and watched the numbers light up.

Just past midnight. Right on schedule.

Cautiously he crawled to the edge of the truckbed, lifted the tarp a few inches, and poked his head out.

Ahead of the truck a long line of red taillights twisted along the streets. In back, headlights cut sharply through the night. The column of flatbeds, vans, and canvas-covered floats seemed to go on for miles.

"Owen?" It was Howie's voice beside him. "I'm scared."

Owen moved over to make room. "Me too," he admitted after a moment.

Together they lay on their stomachs, peering out from under the tarp until the cold wind on their faces drove them back into the warmth of the canvas tent.

"I don't care what Mitch says," Howie whispered. "An awful lot of things can go wrong."

"I know," Owen said. "The really tricky stuff hasn't started yet."

Well, he thought with a sigh, it was too late now to wonder if the plan would really work. It had to.

Besides, everything had gone smoothly so far. The rest of it would be okay too. Sure it would.

Then why was there such a lump of worry in his throat?

"It'll be a cinch to get him hitched to the balloons," he said, as much to himself as to Howie.

"Do you really think they'll be strong enough to lift

him off the ground?" Howie asked.

Owen tried to sound confident. "Sure," he answered. "And once he's up and clear of the buildings, all he has to do is open his wings and fly away. Can you picture it, Howie? There he is, up in the sky—and he's safe because it's too dark for anybody to see him up there. He hangs a left and follows the river down to the harbor, and then he's out over the ocean, and then. . ."

"What if there aren't any plain round balloons in the parade this year?" Howie burst out. "What if there are only the great big character balloons?"

Owen swallowed hard. "The round ones will be there," he said firmly. I hope, he added to himself.

They were silent for a while. Then Howie said, "Y'know something, Owen? First I was real scared of Wyrdryn. He's so big and fierce-looking. But now I'm scared *for* him. In case anything does go wrong, I mean."

"I know," Owen said. After a moment he went on. "I suppose this sounds nuts, Howie, but to me he's not just a dragon anymore. He's . . . my friend."

"It doesn't sound nuts," Howie said.

Owen felt good sharing his feelings with Howie. Talking things over with a real person was better than spilling everything out to Dooley.

The truck lurched as it swung around a corner.

"Where are we?" Gwilym's voice asked from the darkness.

Owen peered out under the tarp. "Going into the

Lincoln Tunnel," he reported. "Under the Hudson River."

"Under a river," Gwilym said with a chuckle. "When I tell *that* to the king, he will think it a jest."

There was a rush of cold air as they came out of the tunnel into Manhattan.

"Hey, you guys," Owen called to the others. "Come see New York City at night!"

The city was dark and quiet on the streets near the river, but lights in the midtown skyscrapers made sparkling patterns against the sky, and the Empire State Building thrust its brightly lit spire high into the night. Beyond low waterfront buildings the river was a streak of silver reflecting the lights in the tall apartment buildings on the New Jersey shore. A jetliner passed high overhead with its wing lights blinking.

"'Tis an astonishment!" the wizard gasped. "Never have I seen such a sight!"

Owen squinted at a street sign. "We're passing Sixty-seventh Street," he said. "Only ten more blocks to go. Heads in!"

Soon the truck slowed to a stop. The door on the passenger side of the cab swung open.

"I'll check the load," Owen heard Grandpa call to the driver. A moment later he was beside the flatbed, pretending to adjust the ropes.

"Everything okay in there?" he asked softly.

Owen lifted the tarp a bit. "Everything's great," he answered. "How come we stopped?"

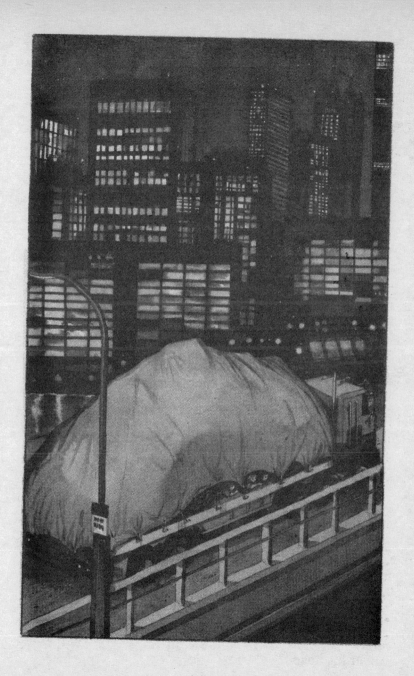

"We're forming up for Seventy-seventh Street," Grandpa explained. "Tell everybody to be ready." He peeled off his windbreaker and handed it to Owen with a smile of encouragement.

Owen watched Grandpa stride back to the cab of the truck, the brass buttons on his red blazer winking in the streetlights. Then he ducked back under the tarp, stuffed Grandpa's windbreaker into the backpack, and crawled over the rough boards of the flatbed in the direction of Wyrdryn's head. "We're almost there, Wyrdryn," he said.

The dragon grunted. "Ohhhhh, Friend Owen, I am so stiff," he moaned.

"I bet you are, but don't move," Owen warned. "Try to think about going home."

The dragon sighed. "A happy thought," he answered. "But alas, inside me I feel a great sadness that jousts with my happiness. 'Tis because I will miss you, Friend Owen. Were it not for you, I would have been alone and forever lost in this strange land."

You still might be, Owen thought. Or worse. He swallowed down the ache in his throat and spoke softly into the dragon's large ear.

"I'll miss you too, Friend Wyrdryn," he said.

As he crawled away toward the others, Owen was glad that in the dark no one could see him rub the back of his hand over his eyes.

As the truck jolted over the bumpy street, the wizard pulled his robe out of his pouch and slipped it over his head.

A police whistle shrilled and the truck stopped again.

"Okay, this one's next," a loud voice said. "Untie the ropes and get the tarp off."

"Wait a minute—hold it," Owen heard his grandfather say in a loud, commanding voice. "We'll need more help for this load—it's heavier than the others. Get those fellows over there."

The men moved off and Grandpa lifted the tarp. "We're almost at the corner of Seventy-seventh Street," he said quickly. "There's a building with a big doorway about fifteen feet to the right. Are you ready? Now!"

Leaving Wyrdryn silent and motionless on the truck, Owen and the others quickly slid out from under the tarp and jumped down to the ground. Seconds later they were hidden in the doorway, blinking at the dazzling scene in front of them.

West Seventy-seventh Street lay like a bright island in the dark streets around it. The whole block alongside the Museum of Natural History, from Columbus Avenue to Central Park West, blazed under powerful floodlights fastened to trees and buildings.

Howie tugged at Owen's sleeve. "I didn't think it would be so lit up," he said in an anxious voice.

Owen was surprised too. All this light might make the whole thing tougher, he thought with a frown.

As the long flatbeds stopped at the head of the block, crews of workers flung back the tarpaulins, pulled off the heavy bundles, and carried them down the street.

141

The street rang with the shouts of the unloading crews and the people leaning out of apartment-house windows to watch.

In the commotion no one paid any attention to the small group in the doorway.

"Look!" Pam cried. "There's Olive Oyl! You can tell even though she's not blown up yet!"

Owen stretched to see the mound of brightly painted rubber and plastic that lay limp and crumpled on the pavement. Its painted eyes stared blankly up at the people in the windows as a crew of workers picked it up and carried it off down the block.

"And I bet that one's Superman," Mitch said. "Hey, this is great!"

The long flatbed trucks clattered away as soon as they were unloaded, and smaller trucks loaded with tanks of helium drove up. Far down the block the inflation crews were already at work. As Owen and his friends watched, Snoopy's smiling face began to rise full and round from the pavement. A web of rope netting went up with him, its dangling ropes swaying as the rest of the huge balloon slowly twitched and quivered into shape.

"Look at all the sandbags hitched to those ropes," Owen said. "They're sure not taking any chances he'll float away."

The wizard touched Owen's arm. "Look there!" he said. "'Tis the turn of Wyrdryn to be unloaded!"

Owen whirled around and felt his heart jump. At

the corner of the street the dragon now lay uncovered on the flatbed. A large crew of men swarmed around him, working at pulling him down to the ground.

"This one's a lot bigger than the others," Owen heard one worker say. "What's it supposed to be, some kind of monster?"

"A dinosaur, I think," another answered. "Look at the long nose and the scales. Jeez, all this plastic—no wonder it's so heavy."

Wyrdryn lay still, acting lifeless. He kept his eyes tightly closed and let his tail and claws flop limply off the sides of the truck as the men tugged at the ropes they had tied around him.

"Staaaand clearrrr!" someone shouted. "Here it comes!"

The dragon's gigantic body rocked heavily on the edge of the flatbed, then slid down onto the street with a loud *whooomp!* and a clatter of spikes, scales, and claws.

Only Owen and the others, watching anxiously from the doorway, could tell that the huge crumpled form on the pavement was alive. Wyrdryn had not flinched or made a sound, and he was breathing so shallowly that he hardly moved.

"Whew," one of the men said. "I sure hope we don't have to move it any farther down the block."

"Oh no, don't worry about that," Grandpa said quickly. "It can stay right here."

Most of the men moved away to unload another

truck, but two of them stayed, walking around the dragon and poking at it.

"Boy, they're makin' 'em fancier every year," one of them said. "Say, mister, y'better get the helium boys over here soon. It's gonna take a long time to blow this baby up."

"Yes, yes, we'll take care of it," Grandpa said.

Owen was relieved when the men went off to join the others, but the good feeling didn't last long.

"Hey, you with the lizard," came a shout. "You didn't gimme your unload order. Bring it over here."

Grandpa looked around, startled. A man leaning out of a small truck on Columbus Avenue was waving a sheaf of papers and beckoning to him.

"Yeah, you," the man called. "I gotta have your signed order—the yellow sheet."

Grandpa ran his fingers over his mustache and frowned. He looked from the man in the truck to Wyrdryn and hesitated.

"C'mon—I got a schedule to follow!" the man yelled impatiently.

Reluctantly Grandpa walked over to the truck, leaving Wyrdryn lying alone in the street.

"The guy in the truck looks mad," Howie said. "What if he finds out there isn't any unload order?"

"I think Grandpa's trying to fake it," Owen said. "See? He's going through his pockets and acting like he's surprised. I bet he's telling the guy it got lost."

"Uh-oh, here comes more trouble," Mitch muttered.

From the other direction two men hauling tanks and hoses came up beside the dragon. They walked around Wyrdryn and ran their hands over the wall of scales as high as they could reach. One of them stepped back, looking puzzled.

"Hoo boy, this is a big one," he said. "You find any valves?"

"Not a one," his partner answered.

"Maybe it gets pumped up through its mouth. Let's take a look."

Owen held his breath as the men bent over the dragon's face. Wyrdryn, chin on the pavement, mouth clamped tightly shut, seemed to be holding his breath too.

"Nope, it doesn't open," one of the men said. "But here's nose holes. Let's give it a try. Full pressure, okay?"

As the hoses swung toward the dragon's face, Owen broke away from the others in the doorway and ran.

"No!" he shouted. "Don't do that!"

It was too late. Firmly in place, the hoses were pumping twin blasts of helium into Wyrdryn's nostrils.

14

WYRDRYN'S HEAD SHUDDERED and jerked back on his neck. Then it shot forward in a roaring sneeze that sent the men tumbling down the street into a pile of sandbags and netting.

"Mommy, that dragon sneezed!" cried a child watching from an apartment window. "And it's blinking its eyes!"

"It's just a rubber balloon, sweetie," her mother answered. "Close the window, it's cold."

Owen and the others crowded around the dragon. "Oh, Wyrdryn, I was scared you'd burst!" Owen cried. "Are you okay?"

"'Twould seem so," Wyrdryn squealed in a high, squeaky voice.

Gwilym looked startled. "What magic has changed his mighty voice into that of a tiny creature?" he asked.

"That's only the helium," Mitch said. "It'll wear off soon."

"The inside of my head buzzes as if with a thousand bees," Wyrdryn squeaked.

"Shh! Close your eyes—those guys are coming back!" Owen cried. "Somebody get Grandpa quick!"

"What's going on here?" one of the men said. "What kind of balloon is this anyway?"

"You almost hurt it—I mean wrecked it!" Owen shouted.

The man pushed Owen aside. "Cool down, sonny, and get out of the way," he said. "Come on, Fred, feed your line in. This time we'll get it right."

"Here now! Stop at once!" It was Grandpa, red-faced and out of breath, shouting as he dashed up and slapped the hose away from Wyrdryn's face.

"Hey, wait a minute!" Fred protested. "You can't do that!"

"This balloon is . . . not to be touched," Grandpa puffed.

The men looked at each other. "Who are you?" the one named Fred asked.

"Crew chief for this balloon," Grandpa said. He drew himself up importantly, smoothed his red jacket, and tapped his clipboard. "Nobody has permission to . . . er, work on it without my orders."

"I never heard of any special deal like that, did you, Charlie?" Fred said to his partner.

Charlie shook his head. "Listen, mister, we've got

orders too. Leave the tanks here, Fred. Let's go get one of the officials."

Owen watched them stride angrily away. "Can we get Wyrdryn up before they come back?" he asked.

"I hope so," Grandpa said. "Do you see any of the balloons we need to lift him?"

Owen shook his head. So far the inflation crews had worked only on the big character balloons. Woody Woodpecker was already up, floating bright and full, six stories tall. As Owen watched him sway gently over the sandbags that moored him to the ground, Kermit the Frog's bright green body rose slowly into the air.

Where were the balloons for Wyrdryn? Owen wondered nervously. Without them the whole plan would fail.

A crowd, gathered behind the railing at the Museum of Natural History, cheered as each big character balloon went up. Now, as a helium crew worked on the crumpled mound of rubber and plastic that was Raggedy Ann, people in the crowd shouted and laughed.

"Hey, look—something's wrong!" Mitch cried.

There was trouble with Raggedy Ann. She hung lopsided in midair, with one of her legs dangling flat and wrinkled beneath her.

"More helium!" Owen heard someone shout. "Get more tanks over here! Stand by the ropes!"

Grandpa peered at the swarms of workers racing to

help. "Good!" he said. "Maybe that will keep them so busy they'll forget about us."

"Pull!" a workman shouted. "No—the other way!"

A groan went up from the crowd. Raggedy Ann's leg had become tangled in its ropes.

"Get that leg free! Cut the rope!"

Knives flashed as the men sawed at the taut rope. Suddenly the strands of rope split apart, and with a loud snap Raggedy Ann's leg smoothed out. The crowd cheered, then screamed, for the huge balloon jerked upward out of balance, tore away from its netting, and slammed into an apartment building. Bumping and scraping, it lurched crazily upward along the wall. On the ground, workers shouted as they struggled with the ropes, pulling in rhythm in a gigantic tug-of-war with the balloon.

A cheer went up from the crowd when Raggedy Ann was finally captured. The noise died to a murmur as the crews worked to tether her over a cluster of sandbags.

Owen peered anxiously down the street. "I don't see those guys coming back," he said, trying to sound hopeful. "Maybe they did forget about Wyrdryn."

He looked at his watch. It had been hours since they had left Hoboken. How much longer would it be until they could get Wyrdryn hitched to the big round balloons and off the ground? And where were the balloons?

The inflation crews worked steadily on. One after

another the giant character balloons rose slowly into the air and floated above the street at their moorings. Near the museum Snoopy swayed in his web of heavy ropes while Raggedy Ann, safe now under her netting, swung slowly back and forth and smiled blankly at him. Superman and Olive Oyl bobbed nearby, straining at their ropes. Owen thought that the big balloons looked impatient for the parade to begin.

He was impatient too, and worry dug into him.

It'll be morning soon, he thought miserably. What then?

There were throngs of people on the block now. Workers in coveralls were running back and forth with armloads of rope and netting, calling to the inflation crews. Parade officials in red jackets like Grandpa's shouted into walkie-talkies. A long line of buses rumbled up Columbus Avenue and stopped at the Seventy-seventh Street corner. Clowns, teddy bears, toy soldiers, and Mother Goose characters climbed down and ran past.

Balloon handlers, Owen knew. They'd be pulling the towropes of the big balloon characters in the parade.

A group of men and women in vegetable costumes stopped to look curiously at Wyrdryn.

"Holy smoke!" said a man dressed as a bunch of broccoli. "What is this, a dragon? I didn't know the parade had a dragon balloon this year."

Grandpa stepped forward. "It's . . . er, new," he said.

"Wow! Look at the size of this thing!" said a tall orange carrot. "How come there hasn't been any publicity about it?"

"It's to be a surprise," Grandpa said.

A girl dressed as a tomato smiled. "It looks great," she said. "I can hardly wait to see it when it's up!"

Me too, Owen thought.

The vegetables ran down the block with the others. All the balloon handlers, Owen noticed, gathered in clusters around section chiefs who were bawling instructions into bullhorns, pointing up at the big balloons, and motioning with their hands. The noise and excitement grew and spread. It would have been fun except for the worry that grew stronger in Owen every minute.

He looked at his watch. After six A.M. already. The balloons they needed should be up by now, shouldn't they? What if Howie was right? What if there wouldn't be any plain round ones in the parade this year?

Grandpa pulled at his mustache and frowned. "Where are they?" he muttered. "Without them . . ."

"Over here!" a man's voice shouted. "This big lizard thing. And here's the guy who wouldn't let us work on it."

Owen spun around. Charlie and Fred were pushing their way through the crowd, and with them was a man with an official-looking badge on his red blazer and a walkie talkie in one hand.

"What's the problem here?" the man asked. "I understand you interfered with the inflation of this balloon."

Grandpa drew himself up and smoothed his own red blazer. "We're waiting for our own crew," he said. "They are specially trained people bringing their own equipment and . . ."

"We don't have time for fancy stuff like that," the man interrupted. "Our men can handle any inflation, even this one. Where are the valves?" He squinted at Wyrdryn, then peered more closely and ran his hand over the dragon's scales.

Owen held his breath. So did Wyrdryn.

Puzzled, the man stepped back. "What is this thing—a dinosaur? a dragon?" he asked. He drew a sheaf of papers from his pocket and flipped through them. "I don't have anything like this listed. What's your position in the line of march?"

"Er . . . uh. . . last," Grandpa stammered.

The official looked Grandpa up and down. Uh-oh, Owen thought to himself. He's sure to see Grandpa doesn't have a badge.

"What's going on here?" the official said. "Where's your identification? Show me the authorization for this balloon."

Grandpa's hands trembled as he patted his pockets. "Well now, I . . . er, seem to have misplaced . . ."

The man was getting impatient now. "Listen, mister," he said, "we've got nine character balloons

152

scheduled for this parade and they're all inflated and ready to go. I don't know who you are or what you're trying to pull, but this thing doesn't get into the parade unless it's on my list. Get it out of here."

"See here, young man," Grandpa sputtered, "you can't . . ."

The official switched on his walkie-talkie. "Joe? Listen, we've got a load for you on Seventy-seventh Street. How soon can you get a truck here—a big one?"

The walkie-talkie squirted out words that Owen couldn't hear plainly.

"An hour?" the official replied. "Come on, make it sooner, will you? And bring a crew with you. We've got a big hunk of junk to get out of here. Yeah, back to Hoboken to the warehouse."

He turned to Grandpa. "Now you tell me who you are and what you're trying to pull," he said. "You can't just . . ."

"*All officials to the reviewing stand,*" the walkie-talkie squawked. "*Report immediately.*"

"I'll deal with you later," the official said. "Meantime, I don't want any trouble or I'll have the cops here and this pile of plastic won't be the only thing that gets hauled away."

"I knew there was something fishy about this," Owen heard Fred say as the three men strode off.

Grandpa's shoulders drooped in defeat as he watched them go. "I guess that was the one thing we didn't think of," he said slowly. "Gwilym, kids . . . I . . . I'm sorry."

Gwilym wrung his hands silently. Tears shone on Pam's cheeks and Howie bit his lip. Even Mitch looked glum.

"Isn't there anything we can do?" Pam managed to say.

"How about if Wyrdryn makes a run for it?" Mitch suggested.

Owen shook his head. There'd be a terrible battle in the streets of Manhattan. It would be his worst fears come true.

No, the whole thing was over. Even now the night was fading away. The sun was coming up golden behind the skyscrapers at the eastern edge of Central Park and the floodlights were being turned off. It was too late. The plan hadn't worked.

How soon before everyone finds out that Wyrdryn's real? Owen wondered. What will happen then?

He dropped down beside the dragon's huge face. "It looks like it's all over, Wyrdryn," he said quietly. "We can't get you back to Wales after all."

The dragon opened his eyes. "You have done your best, Friend Owen," he said. "What will happen to me now?"

"I don't know," Owen answered. "But I'll be there with you. I'll try not to let you get hurt."

"Fear not," the dragon said with a small smile. "I

155

cannot fly, but I can defend myself against hurt. Should there be a battle, you must not be near. You must flee to safety—all of you."

Owen couldn't answer. Beside him Grandpa and the others sat slumped in miserable silence.

How tired Grandpa looks, Owen thought. And old and sad, the way he was before Wyrdryn and Gwilym came. Owen hated the thought of Grandpa going back to his old despairing self.

Suddenly Mitch jumped up. "Look!" he cried.

Far down the street a big balloon was rising in the air. Round and green, it had HAPPY THANKS-GIVING spelled out in glittery letters on its sides. As Owen and the others stared, a red one went up beside it, then a blue one, an orange one, and more.

"Yeah, but now it's too late," Howie said miserably.

Owen scrambled to his feet. "Maybe it isn't," he said. "The truck isn't here yet—we've got one more chance!"

Grandpa looked up at him and a smile lit his face. "You're right!" he said. "We'll have to work fast, though. Gwilym—you stay here close to Wyrdryn. Kids—let's go!"

They hurried down the street, threading their way through the spiderweb of ropes that seemed to cover the whole block, pushing through the crowd of han-dlers dressed as toys and storybook characters.

Underneath the round balloons stood the handlers in vegetable costumes, adjusting towropes and sandbags. The bunch of broccoli seemed to be in charge.

"Say there," Grandpa called, "we've got to move some of these balloons down the block. Will you give us a hand with them?"

The broccoli man stared at him. "Our position is here," he said. "You have written orders for a change?"

"Er . . . no," Grandpa said, "but it's an emergency. There's trouble with—"

"It's the dragon!" Owen burst out. "We need these balloons to get it up in the air!"

The tomato girl's eyebrows went up. "How come it won't float by itself?" she asked.

"There's . . . er, a problem with its internal compartments," Grandpa said. "We must have these balloons!"

The vegetables looked at one another. "Can't do it, mister," the broccoli said. "We're assigned to march in the parade with these balloons. Show me where it says we're supposed to let them be hitched up to some plastic dragon."

"Please!" Pam begged. "We've got to get the dragon off the ground!"

"Aw, come on, don't feel bad," the carrot said. "Lots of times these big fellows don't make it into the parade. A couple of years ago they had to cart Superman away because he sprang a leak."

"Yeah, and one year it was Olive Oyl," a stalk of celery said. "It's tough when it happens, but it's no big deal."

"This *is* a big deal!" Owen cried.

"Sorry, sonny," the broccoli said. "You need balloons? Guess you'll have to blow up your own. There's a pile of extra ones over there."

Owen clenched his fists and looked around desperately as the vegetables turned away. "We could do that!" he cried to Grandpa and the others. "We'll use the tanks the helium men left. Come on!"

Owen and Grandpa grabbed a heap of wrinkled green rubber. It was heavy and they struggled to keep from tripping over its trailing ropes, but they managed to drag it down the street. Behind them Mitch, Pam, and Howie panted as they tugged at an orange one.

"We'll need three more!" Owen shouted as they dumped the balloons beside Wyrdryn. "Let's go get them—hurry!"

It was too late. A long flatbed truck rumbled up and stopped with a hiss of brakes. The driver and three men in coveralls jumped down.

"This the thing we're supposed to haul back to Hoboken?" the driver said. "Okay, guys, let's get it up on the truck."

15

LIFTING WYRDRYN WAS IMPOSSIBLE. He lay limp on the pavement, eyes shut as before, too heavy to move.

"Okay, we'll drag it," said the driver, who seemed to be the foreman in charge. "Get a grip on the tail. Pull!"

Wyrdryn's huge body didn't budge. The men finally had to drop his tail, and it slapped back down on the street with a clatter.

The foreman stepped back shaking his head. "Never saw an uninflated balloon as heavy as this one," he said. "You, Max—round up some help."

As Owen watched Max go down the block, he realized that there was now more noise and excitement everywhere. Across from the museum, on Central Park West, crowds of people waiting for the parade pressed against blue wooden barricades. The roar of motorcycles sounded above their shouts and laughter, and the sound of flutes and trumpets tuning up drifted on the wind.

Red-jacketed parade officials had climbed onto a high wooden stand at the museum corner, and now the shrill squawks and whistles of a public address system cut through the noise on the street and bounced off the buildings.

"Attention all units! Attention all units!" the Grand Marshal's voice boomed.

"Listen!" Mitch said. "It must be parade time!"

"Celebrities—take your places on the floats, please. All skating clowns up front. Balloons, stand by."

Down the block, workers pulled the nets off the giant character balloons and removed the sandbags. The costumed handlers held fast to the balloons' swaying towropes, waiting. Under the round balloons the vegetables waited too.

"Floats and marching bands—keep your units fifty paces apart," the Grand Marshal's voice said. *"Give the balloons plenty of space. Float drivers, keep it slow and smoooooth. Drum majors, be sure to wait for your signals. All units in place! All units in place! Stand by!"*

"Gosh, isn't it exciting!" Pam said.

Owen turned away. The parade didn't matter. It hadn't mattered in the first place. It was just that this was the only place where there were helium balloons big enough to get Wyrdryn off the ground. But they

160

hadn't been able to get the balloons hitched to him.

The whole plan had failed.

All that was left was what he had dreaded. Wyrdryn would end up in a zoo or in a big bloody battle that would leave him—and a lot of people—dead.

He swallowed the ache in his throat and turned back to watch the men straining to lift Wyrdryn. There were ten of them now, among them some who had worked on Raggedy Ann, and although they managed to lift either the front of the dragon or his hindquarters, it was impossible to get all of him up at the same time.

Mitch couldn't resist a wisecrack. "This is a job for Superman!" he muttered in a low, dramatic voice.

"Yeah," Pam agreed. "Too bad he's only a balloon."

Owen stared at his friends. Suddenly he turned and tugged at Grandpa.

"See if you can get the men to hitch on the round balloons!" he hissed into Grandpa's ear.

Grandpa looked startled. Then his eyes lit up and he nodded in understanding.

"Right you are!" he whispered back with a grin. He smoothed his mustache, straightened his shoulders under the red jacket, and stepped up to the sweating foreman.

"Well now," he said, "it seems as if more than muscle power might be needed here. Would it help if you were to attach some balloons and let the helium do the work of lifting?"

The foreman thought it over. "It's a crazy idea," he said finally, "but it might work."

"Yeah," one of the other men agreed. "Then all we'd have to do is tow it over to the truck, cut the ropes, and drop it on."

"Good thinking," Grandpa said. "Well now, there are two uninflated balloons right here, and others just down the block. And here are helium tanks left by two gentlemen a while ago."

"Hey, Mike—Harry!" the foreman yelled. "Go down the block and bring back a couple of uninflated balloons—the round ones with Happy Thanksgiving on them."

Owen felt Grandpa's hand tighten on his arm as they watched the men drag over the balloons and fasten the ropes to Wyrdryn's legs and tail.

"Leave plenty of rope for towing," the foreman ordered. "Okay, take those tanks and fill 'em up!"

A red balloon with glittering HAPPY THANKS-GIVING letters rose into the air over Wyrdryn's tail. As its rope twanged taut the dragon's tail lifted high off the ground and hung down in a long, drooping coil.

"That's more like it!" the foreman shouted. "Get going on those front legs! Hurry up!"

Soon more balloons were floating in the air above Wyrdryn. Owen could see the ropes cutting into the dragon's hide beneath the great leathery scales. Still, in spite of the tremendous pull of the balloons, the only part of Wyrdryn off the ground was his tail.

Down the block, on the high wooden stand at the corner, the Grand Marshal began the countdown for the parade.

"TENNNN—NIIIINE—EIGHT—"

Hundreds of people took up the chant and sent it rippling farther along to the thousands lining the streets, but Owen hardly heard it as he watched the men struggle with Wyrdryn.

"Now—all together—LIFT!" the foreman shouted.

"Owen!" Howie whispered anxiously. "If they get him on the truck they'll take him away!"

Owen gave Howie a reassuring grin. "They'll never get him on that truck," he whispered back. "Once he's up, he can break free and fly away, just as we planned!"

But Wyrdryn's body did not move.

"SEVVVEN—SIXXXX—"

"Geez!" one of the men panted. "Is this thing glued down or something?"

"More balloons! Get those back legs up!" the fore-man shouted.

"What's the matter here?" It was the official in the red jacket, out of breath and impatient.

"We can't get this thing off the ground," the fore-man said. "It weighs a ton."

"Well, I want it out of here fast. We've got to clear the street," the official said angrily. "If you can't lift it, then take it apart and load it on in pieces."

"You mean cut it up?"

"That's exactly what I mean," the official snapped.

"Find the seams and rip it up. Hurry!"

"FIIIVE—FOURRR—THREEE—"

Knives flashed—the same knives that had released Raggedy Ann's crumpled leg.

"No!" Owen screamed, but the blades slashed into the flesh beneath the dragon's scales.

Wyrdryn's eyes snapped open, gleaming with anger. It was too much. The long hours of lying stiff on the hard pavement, the indignity of being called a hunk of junk, and now this!

He leaped up with a fearsome roar. There was a long, loud ripping sound, as if a huge piece of cloth were tearing apart, and the dragon disappeared into a thick, swirling mist.

"TWO—ONE—PARAAAADE!"

A roar went up from the crowd. The drums of the first band thumped. Dozens of clowns on roller skates and skateboards swooped off in the lead. Behind them the motorcycle policemen gunned their engines, swung into a precise row across the broad avenue, and set off down the parade route.

But Owen knew none of it. He ran through the mist, his arms flailing as he groped for the dragon.

There was nothing there.

"He's gone!" he cried. "Oh, Wyrdryn, where are you?"

"Friend Owen!" a deep voice rumbled. "Look you up this way!"

Owen blinked up through the shreds of mist. There, swaying under the balloons, hung the dragon, rising into the sunlight that slanted down on Seventy-seventh Street.

"He is free of the spell at last!" the wizard cried. "'Tis a wondrous turn of events!"

"But you're not up there with him!" Owen shouted. "Wyrdryn—wait for Gwilym!" He grabbed one of the dangling ropes, but the balloons lifted Wyrdryn higher and the rope slipped through his hands, burning his skin.

"Grab those ropes!" the foreman shouted to his crew. "Pull it toward the truck!"

Wyrdryn's lunge had knocked two of the workmen down, and they seemed dazed as they stared at the others tugging on the ropes.

"Boy, I thought Raggedy Ann was a tough one, but this beats everything!" one of them said as he got to his feet.

"Yeah," another said. "I must be nuts—I thought I heard it talk!"

Gwilym dashed forward and shouted up to the dragon. "Quickly, Wyrdryn! Raise me onto your back! We must begin our journey!"

The foreman pushed him aside. "Get out of the way, Pop," he ordered. "And stay back. We've got work to—hey, look out!"

The men ducked as one of the dragon's great paws swept down toward the ground. Swiftly Wyrdryn scooped up the wizard and swung him up onto his scaly shoulder. With another roar he twisted his head around and raked the workmen with his gleaming yellow eyes.

The men froze, locked motionless in dragonstare.

Owen grinned with delight. He cupped his hands and called up to the dragon, "Remember, Wyrdryn—straight up till you clear the buildings! Then unfurl your wings and fly south to the harbor, and—Wyrdryn, are you listening?"

Band music blared from the parade and Wyrdryn thrust his head out, ears quivering and eyes sparkling. The outer ribs of his wings unfolded, and with small, firm strokes he launched himself forward, toward the parade corner.

"No, not that way!" Owen shouted. *"Go up, Wyrdryn! You're going in the wrong direction!"*

Desperately Owen and the others grabbed the towropes and tugged, but it was useless. Pulling the balloons that kept him afloat, the dragon surged through the air along Seventy-seventh Street as Owen and the others clung to the ropes, afraid to let go.

"Make him stop!" Pam cried as the dragon dragged them along over piles of netting and sandbags. "He's going to mess everything up!"

"Can't . . . hold . . . him . . . back!" Grandpa panted. "He's too strong!"

"Wyrdryn!" Owen cried. "Where are you going?"

"To the Grand Procession!" Wyrdryn answered, his eyes fixed steadily on the corner. "'Tis my wish to be part of it!"

"Oh nooooo!" Howie wailed.

Owen fought down a sharp stab of panic.

Wyrdryn in the parade? All by himself, without a crew of handlers? People would be sure to realize he was a real live dragon, and then what?

There was only one thing to do.

"Don't drop the ropes!" he shouted to the others. "We have to go with him into the parade!"

"How 'bout that, Howie?" Mitch said with a grin. "We told you this would be some Thanksgiving!"

"Gee," Pam said, "all the time we pretended he was a dragon balloon I never thought we'd be in the parade!"

"It seems we don't have any choice," Grandpa said. He flung his head back and shouted up to the dragon. "Keep your wings quiet, Wyrdryn, and let us tow you. And please—you too, Gwilym—try to pretend you belong in the parade!"

Wyrdryn's mouth pulled back in a broad smile and he nodded with pleasure as he settled his wings back onto his body. On his back the wizard leaned forward intently. There was no need for him to pretend. Like the dragon, he too had been swept up in the music and excitement, and now he looked as eager as Wyrdryn to be part of the parade up ahead. Above them the balloons bobbed gently, their Happy Thanksgiving messages glittering in the sun.

Now that they were towing the dragon, Owen realized how sore his hands were. It didn't matter, though. He and the others were Wyrdryn's crew now, and they mustn't let anything stop them.

168

He looked nervously around. Behind them, the workmen still stood frozen. Up ahead, the crowd of onlookers had moved to the corner to watch the bands and floats flowing past. The cleanup crews were busy loading netting, sandbags, and empty helium tanks onto carts. They were paying no attention to a red-jacketed man helping a small group tow what seemed like just another character balloon.

Maybe they could make it work. If not . . .

"There goes Woody Woodpecker!" Mitch cried as the big balloon, its red topknot flashing bright in the sun, swung around the corner into the line of march. The other character balloons moved up, bobbing against their towropes as they waited their turns.

A sudden thump overhead jolted Owen off his feet. Wyrdryn had bumped into Olive Oyl and Superman.

"A thousand pardons, madam," the dragon said with a courtly nod as he swept past. "Kind sir, do forgive my haste."

Before the startled handlers could respond, Wyrdryn and his crew surged ahead.

Now Owen could see more of the parade. A band strode past in a mass of flashing batons, bright uniforms, and gleaming instruments. Behind it rolled Cinderella's float, with its pumpkin-shaped coach and white plastic horses. Wyrdryn gave an excited twitch when he caught sight of Cinderella herself, dressed in a billowing white ball gown that sparkled with jewels.

"Owen, Pam—listen, all of you!" Grandpa shouted.

"Don't pay attention to anything people say or do. Whatever happens, KEEP GOING!"

Owen's hands tightened on the rope and a shiver raced down his back. He managed to flash a smile at Howie.

"Hang on!" he shouted. "Here we gooooooo!"

16

A ROAR OF SURPRISE went up from the crowd as Owen and the others swung the dragon around the corner into the parade. Children holding small bright balloons jumped up and down, screaming in mock fear as they pointed up at Wyrdryn.

The startled voices of the Grand Marshal and his staff came sputtering over the public address system.

"Hey—what's that? We don't have any dragon scheduled in the parade!"

"Call parade headquarters, quick! Find out what this is all about!"

"You there with the dragon—you can't do this! STOP!"

There was no stopping. Owen and the others marched briskly along as if they heard nothing more than the cheers of the crowd. Tall and smiling in his red jacket, Grandpa nodded to the right and left as the dragon sailed down the avenue away from the Grand Marshal's stand.

"We did it!" Mitch shouted. "Way to go, Wyrdryn!"

The round balloons held Wyrdryn firmly aloft as he floated steadily along. He swung his huge head from side to side and smiled with delight as he looked out at the towers of the city and the glittering parade that wound before him. Gwilym smiled too, sitting proud on his scaly seat and waving as he and Wyrdryn passed over the heads of the thousands of people who jammed the sidewalks shouting, cheering, laughing, and pointing up at the gigantic dragon being drawn through the air.

"Look!" Pam shouted. "Wyrdryn's on TV!"

Television camera crews stationed along the way were swinging their cameras away from the Cinderella float to focus on the dragon.

"Bet they've never seen a parade like this one!" Mitch shouted. "Do you s'pose we're on TV too?"

"I hope so," Pam shouted as she flashed a silver grin at the cameras.

Wyrdryn skimmed along smoothly as they rounded Columbus Circle and marched down Broadway. Owen's arms ached. His hands were sore and his face felt scoured by the wind, but he strode along in a brisk rhythm. It was wonderful to see everyone so happy. Grandpa marched proudly, smiling and nodding to the throngs of people on both sides of the street. Mitch and Pam were capering, and even Howie was mugging a little, as if being in the parade were something he did every year.

Well, things didn't work out exactly as I planned, Owen thought, but this is even better!

"Hey, Mitch!" he shouted. "Isn't this a great parade!"

Mitch grinned. "It sure beats a bunch of ribbons tied to an ox!" he shouted back.

At an intersection Owen caught a glimpse of a street sign. Fifty-fifth Street.

"Grandpa!" he shouted. "When does Wyrdryn take off?"

"The parade ends in front of Macy's at Thirty-fourth Street," Grandpa shouted back. "When we get there, we'll release the ropes and away he goes!"

It was harder to keep Wyrdryn on a straight course now. Smiling his broad dragon smile, he twisted back and forth as he bowed graciously at people watching the parade from windows and balconies on both sides of the street. A cluster of stone gargoyles carved high on the side of a hotel caught his eye, and he nosed over to peer curiously at them.

"I bet he thinks they're friends or relations," Mitch remarked. "Come on, Wyrdryn, stay with it, will ya?"

With a regretful glance backward Wyrdryn floated past the gargoyles, then gasped and reared back in surprise as he caught sight of himself reflected in a tall glass building.

"He thinks it's another dragon!" Grandpa shouted. "Gwilym, quick—tell him about mirrors!"

Owen saw the wizard lean forward and call urgently to the dragon. With a puzzled look Wyrdryn stared at his reflection, then grinned with pleasure as he preened and posed while Owen and the others pulled him past the wall of glass.

"I wish he wouldn't gawk at everything," Pam complained. "My hands are sore."

"It won't be long now," Owen told her as they approached Times Square. His own hands hurt so much that he wrapped the rope around his arm several times.

It was worse when they reached Times Square, with its giant billboards. With a jerk of surprise and delight Wyrdryn flung himself toward one of the huge signs, then twisted toward another as Owen and the others struggled to keep him moving forward in the parade.

"Gee, I wish he wouldn't act like such a tourist," Mitch yelled as they zigzagged out of Times Square and marched down Broadway once more.

"Wyrdryn!" Grandpa shouted. "Soon we'll come to another open square. When I tell you, open your wings and fly straight on to the harbor. Happy landings!"

Wyrdryn nodded. High on his back Gwilym leaned over and gave the okay sign.

Just a few more blocks, Owen thought. And then it'll all be over.

Herald Square was coming up fast. As he peered around Cinderella's float, Owen could see Macy's department store, its facade bright with strings of lights. On the other side of the square, on a high reviewing stand, loudspeakers boomed out the voices of television commentators describing performers who sang and danced before the cameras.

"Look at Woody Woodpecker!" Howie shouted. Like the other character balloons, Woody Woodpecker had been towed out of the line of march onto a side street and hauled down. As they marched past, Owen and the others caught a glimpse of a drooping red topknot being swiftly deflated. Snoopy and Raggedy Ann already lay collapsed on the pavement.

Crowds of people had surged past the wooden barricades to watch, and a group of mounted policemen came clattering up to block the entrance to the street. In one startled moment the horses caught sight of the dragon. Eyes wide, they reared up, snorting and whinnying as they pawed the air.

Wyrdryn was startled too. "Knights on war-horses!" he roared. "They have come to attack me!" With a loud snap he flung open his wings and shot upward.

Howie and Mitch crashed into each other and dropped their ropes. As they tumbled to the pavement, they fell in a heap next to Grandpa and Pam.

"Owen—let go!" Grandpa screamed.

But Owen, the rope wrapped around his arm, was swept upward, dangling helplessly beneath the soaring dragon.

A wild tangle of ropes whipped against Owen as Wyrdryn swooped over Herald Square. Unaware that anyone was hanging underneath, the dragon circled higher and higher while Gwilym pounded on his scaly back and shouted frantically in Welsh.

Finally the dragon peered down, startled.

"Friend Owen!" he roared. With a swift gesture he reached down a massive front paw and scooped Owen into it, rope and all.

Owen lay in the cup of claws, his knees drawn up to his chin and his whole body shaking with cold and fright. He struggled to catch his breath, and after a moment he peered out carefully between two of the claws.

Wyrdryn was flying in a wide circle over the top of Macy's and the buildings across the square. His wings pulsed in a powerful rhythm, and the bright balloons tied to his legs and tail bobbed behind him. On the ground the parade had come to a ragged stop. Everyone was staring up at the dragon.

Owen gulped and looked away. He managed to sit up and unwrap the rope from his arm. With cold, shaking hands he wound it several times around his waist and tied it as firmly as he could. If he slipped out of Wyrdryn's grasp, at least he wouldn't fall all the way to the ground.

The loudspeakers on the reviewing stand sputtered with the excited voices of the TV announcers.

"Folks, in the sixty years since these Thanksgiving Day parades began, nobody's ever seen anything like the show

that is going on here today!"

"That's right! How can they ever top this wonderful bal-loon!"

"Can you call it a balloon? It looks more like a . . . well, a flying machine made out of some kind of plastic."

"And it's some kind of mystery too! The schedule we were given doesn't list a dinosaur—no, I think it's a dragon, with a performer dressed like a magician riding on its back. Well, whatever it is, it's giving us a sensational show!"

"And how did you like that aerial act?"

"Better than anything I've ever seen in a circus! What a thrill to see that acrobat pretend to be pulled off the ground by the rope!"

Pretend? Owen shivered and gave the knot another yank. Suddenly he felt a jolt as Wyrdryn swung his paw upward.

"Up with you, Friend Owen," the dragon said, "to a seat near Gwilym!"

Owen gulped. Climb out onto Wyrdryn's back while they were whizzing along fifteen stories above the street?

"Take my hand, lad!" the wizard shouted as he leaned forward.

With one hand still clutching the rope and the other firmly in Gwilym's grasp, Owen managed to crawl onto Wyrdryn's scaly back and settle between two spikes.

On the street below the crowd went wild with excitement.

"What will these sensational acrobats do next?" the TV

commentator shouted. *"Look—the small one has climbed up on the dragon's back! He's sitting right in front of the magician! Fasten your seat belt, fella!"*

"All you folks watching at home on your TV's—the camera's zooming in for a close-up shot of these amazing performers! There they are—now you can see them up close—the magician in his robelike costume and a long gray beard . . ."

". . . And the other one! Hey, it looks like a kid! It is! Folks, that acrobat up there is only a child! Can't be much more than about ten years old!"

"Must come from a family of circus performers! What a talented youngster! Where in the world did Macy's ever find an act like this!"

Wyrdryn banked into a turn and Owen clutched the spike in front of him. He peered over the dragon's side and tried to find Grandpa and the others in the swirling crowd below, but it was no use. It looked as if half the world were in Herald Square right now—shouting, laughing, and pointing up at the circling dragon.

Wyrdryn made another turn and zigzagged over the parade floats.

"Wyrdryn—where are you going?" Owen shouted.

"I am searching for—ah, there she is!" the dragon cried. His eyes sparkled and he made a sudden dip sideways.

"Look below, Friend Owen!" he cried as he pointed a long claw at the Cinderella float. "I have found a princess after all in this land of yours! And I will take her home with me! Hold on!"

As the dragon bore down on her, Cinderella threw her arms up over her head and screamed in terror.

"Wyrdryn, no!" Owen cried. "That's not a real princess! It's only a plain person dressed up like one! Leave her alone!"

Wyrdryn swept past and peered at the shrieking Cinderella. Tiara askew and face smeared with makeup, she was scrambling to the edge of the float and jumping down. The skirt of her shimmering white gown ripped, revealing light-blue ski pants underneath.

With a sudden tail flick Wyrdryn soared upward again.

"'Tis so, she is no true princess," he grumbled. "Imagine behaving with such lack of royal dignity at the mere sight of a dragon."

As they flew past the remnants of the parade, Wyrdryn twisted his head around toward Owen. "Then what of you?" he asked suddenly. "Will *you* come home with me?"

Owen blinked in surprise, and Gwilym looked startled too. "For shame, Wyrdryn," the wizard said. "A person is not a souvenir."

The dragon's yellow eyes flashed. "I would not have you be a souvenir," he said with a long, serious look at Owen. "I invite you as my friend."

A shiver of excitement curled down Owen's back.

Not to say good-bye to Wyrdryn, but to go back through the centuries with him!

To see kings and castles, to cheer while knights in clanking armor jousted in tournaments—maybe even to wear a suit of armor himself some day!

He could watch Gwilym make magic spells that really worked, and listen to bards sing their stories of glorious deeds. What an adventure it would be to live in the dragon's own world!

In that world there would be no Mrs. Yellen and no Marve Parker.

But . . . there would be no Mom and Dad either. And no Grandpa. No way to be friends with Mitch or Howie or Pam.

Yet if he didn't go, he'd never see Wyrdryn again.

They flew on in silent circles, higher and higher over the tall buildings that crowded between the glistening rivers, and Owen tried to make up his mind. As they made a graceful loop around the Empire State Building, Wyrdryn turned his head to look at Owen again.

"What say you, Friend Owen?" the dragon asked. "Will you come home with me?"

17

OWEN BIT HIS LIP. "I can't go home with you, Wyrdryn," he said at last. "I'm sorry, but. . . home for me is here."

Wyrdryn turned his face away and dipped his head. Although his wings beat on steadily, Owen felt his body heave in a sigh.

Gwilym gave Owen's shoulder a warm squeeze. "We must set you to earth, lad," he said. "Know you where it can be done safely?"

"There's a park at the harbor," Owen replied, "and from there you can fly straight out to sea."

The wizard rose up in his seat. "South to the harbor, Wyrdryn!" he directed. "Make for the park at water's edge."

Wyrdryn lifted his head and swung toward the tip of Manhattan. They rounded the TV antenna on top of the World Trade Center and flew past the last tall towers of New York City.

There! Straight ahead was the harbor, its water

gleaming like silver. Freighters stood at anchor and ferryboats glided across the broad bay, their decks crowded with people staring up at the approaching dragon.

Wyrdryn made a wide circle of the harbor and flung a startled look at the Statue of Liberty.

"Another creature locked in a spell!" he cried. "Friend Owen, one day you must think of a way to release this giant queen!"

Owen clung anxiously to the spike in front of him. Could Wyrdryn manage to set him down safely on land? A crowd was already gathering at Battery Park. If there were police there, it might not be safe for the dragon to fly close to the shore. He hoped he wouldn't be dropped into the water. It looked soft and sparkling, but it was November cold.

"Friend Owen, is your rope secure?" the dragon called.

Owen tested the knot. "Yes!" he called back.

"Then hold tight—and be not afraid!"

With a sudden movement, Wyrdryn flipped his tail to one side and snapped a blast of flame toward the orange balloon tied to it. The balloon burst with a tremendous *pop* and Owen felt Wyrdryn's whole body jerk in the air, then level out.

Two more bursts of flame popped the green and red balloons, and Owen clung tightly to his spike as Wyrdryn turned his head from side to side and sent spurts of red flame toward the last balloons.

It's like riding a bucking bronco! Owen thought.

All around him the ropes sizzled into ashes, while long shreds of bright-colored rubber floated down toward the water, trailing bits of glittering Happy Thanksgiving messages.

"Well done!" the wizard shouted. "Now, Wyrdryn, to our last task. Fare you well, lad."

Carefully Owen climbed into the dragon's outstretched paw. The great curved claws closed around him and Wyrdryn swooped toward the park at the edge of the harbor. Halfway there the tilt of his wings changed. Like twin black fans they moved straight up and down now, whirring powerfully and moving him slowly over the last stretch of water. Owen tensed and peered anxiously out between the claws. Suddenly he saw a tall man in a red blazer push through the crowd, waving both arms in the air.

"It's Grandpa!" he shouted.

Howie and Mitch and Pam were there too, jumping up and down, waving their arms and shouting.

"They're all here to say good-bye to you!" Owen shouted up to the dragon.

Wyrdryn looked down into his paw. "And you, Friend Owen—you will say good-bye to me too," he said sadly.

Owen gulped. "Yes," he answered. "But I'll never forget you."

"Down you go, lad!" the wizard said. "Hold the rope!"

Owen held it. Wyrdryn spread open his claws and tipped him out. The crowd at the waterfront screamed, but the rope pulled tight around Owen's waist and held. He dangled underneath the swiftly whirring wings, closer and closer to the water beneath him as the dragon neared the shore.

People scrambled backward, but Grandpa darted forward and grabbed Owen's legs. The dragon flicked a delicate curve of flame at the rope, and Owen slid into Grandpa's arms.

Then, with a powerful rush of wings, Wyrdryn gave a sudden flip and soared swiftly up over the harbor.

Snug in Grandpa's arms, Owen saw the wizard wave at them, then shout into Wyrdryn's ear. Wyrdryn nodded and swooped down low. Gwilym leaned over and plucked a large piece of red rubber out of the water with the tip of his magic wand. For a moment the dragon hovered almost motionless in the bright blue sky, while the wizard held up the piece of tattered balloon like a banner.

It was one glittering word.

THANKS, it said.

Then Wyrdryn pointed his head upward and spouted a tremendous burst of flame. Orange, red, and hot shining yellow, it burst from his mouth with a thunderous roar, rose high into the air, and exploded into a huge shower of glistening sparks.

"Look at the fireworks!" a child shouted.

In the midst of the dazzling cascade Wyrdryn

wheeled about, swooped gracefully over the Verrazano Narrows Bridge, and headed out to sea.

A swarm of people buzzed about with questions, but Grandpa shoved Owen and the others into the taxi he had waiting. "This gentleman will drive us to Hoboken," he said. "We'll pick up my car there and head for home."

As the taxi drove out of the park, Owen and the others looked back at the harbor. The dragon and the wizard were faraway specks in the sky now.

Howie squinted into the sun. "What if they don't make it?" he said.

"They'll make it," Owen said, and he settled into the warm curve of Grandpa's arm.

"Wow," Pam said with a sigh, "I'm totally beat."

"Me too," Mitch said. "And hungry. I could eat a whole Thanksgiving turkey all by myself. Hey, Owen, it must have been fun flying around on top of Wyrdryn. Were you scared?"

Owen smiled. "I've been scared ever since I found him in back of the garage," he admitted.

Grandpa's arm tightened gently around him. "There was a lot to be scared about," Grandpa said.

There was silence for a moment. Then Grandpa went on quietly, "I was scared long before Wyrdryn showed up."

Owen knew what he meant. He'd been scared of

life without Grandma, and that had made him lose his way. But helping Wyrdryn had changed all that.

"You know what?" Howie said. "I'm glad Wyrdryn's gone, but I'm glad it all happened."

"Yeah," Mitch agreed. "There's nothing like having a fire-breathing, ox-eating dragon around."

"And a wizard," Grandpa added. "He was here at just the right time."

Like good old Dooley, Owen thought. Here when I needed him. But now . . .

Owen looked around at his friends. His hands hurt and he wanted to sleep for a million years, but he couldn't help feeling happy.

"Hey, you guys," he said. "It's a great Thanksgiving, isn't it!"

"You bet!" Howie said. "Totally great!"